"You haven't slept. Do me a favor and try to close your eyes."

He pulled his hand back, gathered up used supplies and tossed them into the garbage.

"Okay." She bit back a yawn as he turned off the light.

He hadn't wanted to admit just how freaked out he'd been when he saw that she'd been shot. He'd stayed calm for her benefit.

Dylan couldn't even think about losing her, too. *Where'd that come from?*

Thankfully, Samantha would be all right.

"Will you come over here?" Her sweet, sleepy voice wasn't helping with his arousal.

The room had just enough light to see big objects without being able to tell what they were. His own adrenaline was fading, leaving him fatigued.

He walked over and sat down. She took his hand. Hers was so small in comparison, so soft.

"Will you lie next to me?" she asked in that sexy sleepy voice. "Just until I fall asleep?"

TEXAS TAKEDOWN

Barb Han

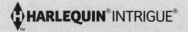

My deepest thanks go to my editor, Allison Lyons, and agent, Jill Marsal. The chance to work with both of you is truly a gift.

There are three people in this world who always inspire me, bring me joy and laughter, and teach me to be the best person I can be. I love you, Brandon (Hook'em Horns), Jacob and Tori.

To my husband, John, because you are the best part of all of it.

ISBN-13: 978-0-373-69863-9

Texas Takedown

Copyright © 2015 by Barb Han

Recycling programs for this product may not exist in your area.

HARLEQUIN®
www.Harlequin.com

Printed in U.S.A.

Barb Han lives in north Texas with her very own hero-worthy husband, three beautiful children, a spunky golden retriever/standard poodle mix and too many books in her to-read pile. In her downtime, she plays video games and spends much of her time on or around a basketball court. She loves interacting with readers and is grateful for their support. You can reach her at barbhan.com.

Books by Barb Han

Mason Ridge

Texas Prey
Texas Takedown

The Campbells of Creek Bend

Witness Protection
Gut Instinct
Hard Target

Harlequin Intrigue

Rancher Rescue

Harlequin Intrigue Noir

Atomic Beauty

CAST OF CHARACTERS

Samantha Turner—She goes into hiding when the Mason Ridge Abductor returns and sets his sights on her. He's supposed to be dead and the case closed, but she's sure it's him. When Dylan shows up to help and then his daughter goes missing, Samantha blames herself. And she'll stop at nothing to reunite the man she's falling for with his daughter.

Dylan Jacobs—Sparks fly whenever he's near Samantha, and he feels a connection with her— a connection someone wants permanently broken. When his three-year-old daughter is kidnapped, he'll have to decide how much he's willing to gamble to find her, or if he's willing to trade one life for another.

Maribel Jacobs—This three-year-old has taken Dylan's world by storm. When she goes missing, he'll do whatever it takes to get her back.

Henry Turner—He's gone into hiding, but why? What does he really know about the Mason Ridge Abductor?

Thomas Kramer—He was part of the breakdown crew for the Renaissance Festival that occupies Mason Ridge for a week every summer. He's been identified as the Mason Ridge Abductor, and he's supposed to be dead.

Charles Alcorn—Why do all roads keep leading to the richest man in the county?

Bearded—He works security for Alcorn and shows up at the darnedest times.

Bright Guy One—Another one of Alcorn's security men who seems to be in the wrong place.

Sheriff Brine—Is his association with a prominent family blinding his judgment on Mason Ridge's most notorious case and the incidents that have happened since?

Chapter One

Difficult didn't begin to cover the past year for Dylan Jacobs. Not only had he discovered that he was a father, but he'd learned the mother who'd kept the baby from him was terminally ill. He'd wanted to be angry with her on both counts, but his frustration had died on the vine with every step toward the hospital where she lay losing her grip on life. And once he'd looked into his daughter's green eyes—a perfect reflection of his—he'd been wrapped around that little girl's finger.

Falling in love with Maribel had been the easy part. She had rosy cherub cheeks, dark curls for days and a laugh brighter than the Texas sun. Caring for a two-year-old who'd just lost everything known to her, everything comfortable, had been harder than his tour in Afghanistan.

What a difference a year made.

Dylan squatted at the end of the hallway just out of sight, listening intently as the sounds of Maribel's electric toothbrush hummed, then died. The pitter-patter of her bare feet on bamboo flooring in the hallway came next. She knew the drill, the same ritual they'd performed every morning since she'd come to live with him in Mason Ridge. She'd be on the lookout, ready to find Da-da.

Her giggle was like spring air, breathing life into everything around her. And he'd been on a certain path of destruction before she came into his life.

The *tap-tap-tap* of her footsteps stopped at the end of the hall. She'd expected to find him by now.

"Da-da."

He rolled and landed with his back against the floor a few feet away, arms spread open.

She jumped, squealed and clapped all at once. A second later, she launched herself on top of him. "Da-da!"

Thanks to reflexes honed by the US Army, he caught her in time.

"Airplane, Da-da," she said. Her *r* came out as a *w*.

Dylan extended his arms and made her fly. "Mrrrrrr, mrrrrrrr."

A knock at the back door interrupted their playtime. It was probably for the best. Maribel shouldn't be late to preschool again. Dylan didn't think he could stomach another disapproving look from Mrs. Applebee. He might not be the most punctual guy when it came to dropping his daughter off at school, but no one could argue his love for the child. Not even stern-faced, disapproving Applebee. She might run a tight ship, but her heart was pure gold. More important, she loved Maribel.

He set his little girl on her feet next to him. "Daddy needs a favor. Go to your room, put on your shoes and grab your backpack."

She planted her balled fist on her little hip and argued for a little more time as a plane.

The knock came louder this time. Dylan didn't like the sense of urgency it carried. "When you get home from school today, I promise. Okay, Bel?"

She pursed her lips and narrowed her gaze.

"And we can have ice cream after," he threw in to tip

the scale in his favor. "You don't want to miss your field trip to Dinosaur Park."

"Ho-kay" came out on a sigh. She turned and bolted toward her room. Toddlers had one speed. It was full tilt.

Dylan popped to his feet in one swift motion and crossed to the kitchen, his muscles still warm from his early-morning push-ups. He liked to get his workout in before Maribel opened her eyes. When she was awake, his full attention was on her, had to be on her. Three-year-olds had no sense of danger.

Only a few people used his back door. He saw his friend Rebecca Hughes through the glass and motioned for her to come inside.

"Everything okay with Shane?" Shane was the younger brother she'd recently located who had been abducted at seven years old. Dylan tried not to think about the fact that Shane had been only four years older than his Maribel when he'd been taken from Mason Ridge and the Hughes family all those years ago. Even so, a bolt of anger flashed through him quicker than a lightning rod and with the same explosive effect.

"He's fine. I'm not here about him." Didn't those words leave a creepy-crawly feeling all over Dylan?

"What is it? Something going on with Brody?" She had reunited with her high school sweetheart, who was one of Dylan's best friends, when the man responsible for kidnapping her and her brother as children had come back for her last month.

She shook her head. "It might not be anything. It's just that Samantha stopped answering her cell phone four days ago. I have a bad feeling."

"You call her father?" he asked.

"Store says he's gone fishing," she supplied. Samantha's father owned the only hardware store in town.

"So you want me to look into it?" Since opening the doors to his security consulting firm last year, he'd taken the occasional missing-person case, none of which had involved a friend's disappearance. He, Rebecca and Samantha had been part of a close-knit group of childhood friends. The group had broken up fifteen years ago when Rebecca and her brother, Shane, had been abducted.

For the past few weeks, everyone in town had been focused on the manhunt for the Mason Ridge Abductor after he'd returned to permanently quiet Rebecca. Her search for her brother had brought her too close to the truth. Thomas Kramer's grip on the community had lasted fifteen years, but luck had finally smiled on the town and they'd gotten him. He wasn't in prison, where he belonged, but he'd been killed in a car crash and that was just as good. Either way, he was no longer a threat.

Dylan thought about his word choice. *Luck?* There was a reason he didn't have a rabbit's foot tucked in his pocket. Hard work was reliable. Luck was for ladies in Vegas at the slot machines. Luck was for people who believed in things they couldn't see. Luck was for pie-in-the-sky dreamers. Dylan was far too practical to fall into that trap. People created their own luck.

With a state-of-the-art computer, a strong network of contacts and skills honed through the military, Dylan didn't have to rely on chance to help his clients.

Even so, he couldn't shake the bad feeling he had about Rebecca's visit.

Maribel bounded into the room, ran straight for Rebecca and wrapped tiny arms around her knees. "Auntie Becca!"

"Hey, baby girl." Rebecca bent down to eye level and then kissed Maribel on the forehead.

The two had become fast friends. A tug Dylan didn't

want to acknowledge stirred his heart. Rebecca was fantastic, don't get him wrong, but he suspected the bond had happened so quickly in part because Maribel missed her mother. He kept Lyndsey's picture on Maribel's nightstand. Maribel kissed the photograph every night before bed and then said good-night to her mother in heaven. It was important that Maribel knew just how much her mother had loved her. Even more important to Dylan was that Maribel knew her mother had wanted her.

On some level, he understood why Lyndsey had kept his daughter from him. He'd been partly to blame, having declared long ago that he never wanted kids or marriage. How many times had he told Lyndsey that parenthood was about the cruelest thing a person could do to a child? Too many.

His wild-child ways hadn't helped any. He had no right to hold on to anger when it came to Lyndsey's decision. She'd been trying to protect her baby.

Dylan never took for granted how very blessed he'd been from the day that little girl had come into his life. His only regret was that he hadn't known sooner, that Lyndsey hadn't realized how much being present in his child's life would mean to him. Had he been that much of a jerk?

The short answer? Yes.

He had to have been. Lyndsey would've trusted him otherwise. He couldn't blame her, either. How many times when they'd lain in bed in the mornings had he said their life was perfect the way it was? Dozens? Hundreds? He'd been so adamant that he'd almost convinced himself, too.

Down deep, he'd wanted a family of his own but he'd never have been able to admit that to himself. He'd always figured that he'd jack it up. History repeating itself and all that. Except the one thing Dylan knew above all was that he was nothing like his parents. He'd gone to great lengths to ensure it.

And yet he couldn't help but think he'd failed Lyndsey. Because of his stubborn streak, she'd gone through her pregnancy alone. Then she'd had a baby by herself. To top it off, she'd spent the first two years of Maribel's life without any help from him.

He could give himself the cop-out all day long that he'd have done better by Lyndsey if he'd known. Still didn't ease the sting of feeling as if he'd let her down in the worst possible way when she needed him. And then, before he could make any of it right, she'd died.

At least she hadn't done that alone—he'd made certain. He'd maintained a bedside vigil during her last days. She'd been in a coma and couldn't speak. The only thing she could do was squeeze his hand when he apologized for letting her down.

Dylan sighed sharply. Those memories had been packed away and stowed deep. So why were they resurfacing?

And how ridiculous did his point of view seem to him now? His life wouldn't be complete without that little rug rat. Maturity was on his side. But he never would have turned Maribel away. Lyndsey couldn't have known. She'd believed the wilder side of Dylan.

He turned to Rebecca. "I need to run Maribel to school and then I'll make a few calls. You want to stick around and wait? Coffee's fresh."

"I wish I could stay. We've got a colt that's in trouble and Brody has his hands full. I better get back and help with the other horses." She'd moved in with Brody after rekindling their romance, and they'd be announcing a wedding date any day now. Together they made a great team running his horse rehabilitation center, and the work looked to agree with her. Or maybe it was just the fact that she'd found someone who could make her happy.

Dylan had more pressing matters to think about than the complications having another female in his life would bring. His three-foot-tall angel kept him on the brink of exhaustion.

"I can take Maribel to school if you want. It's on my way home," she offered.

Dylan figured that was Rebecca's way of saying she hoped he'd get started looking for Samantha right away.

Maribel was already jumping up and down, clapping her hands.

He nodded to Rebecca, even though he'd miss being the one to take his little girl to school. His part-time nanny, Ms. Anderson, usually picked up Maribel in the afternoons. She cooked suppers and stayed as long as Dylan needed her around. Said she enjoyed keeping busy after being widowed at the young age of sixty. When he'd hired her, she'd volunteered to come in first thing in the mornings, too, but Dylan had refused. He couldn't give up being the one to wake Maribel. His daughter might've come out of nowhere a year ago, but she was here to stay, in his home and in his heart. Dylan couldn't imagine his life any other way.

Between Ms. Anderson, Mrs. Applebee and Maribel, Dylan had plenty of estrogen in his life.

Having his own business allowed him to work from home a lot of the time and set his own schedule for the most part. But there were occasions when he had to be away overnight. He appreciated Ms. Anderson's flexibility.

"I'll call the headmaster and give up my volunteer spot on the field trip."

"I'd hate for you to do that," Rebecca said.

"I have a few other things to do today anyway. And I'm pretty sure Applebee could use a break from me. There's a wait list for these trips. This'll give another parent a shot."

Maribel frowned.

"Hey, I worked the past two. It's good to share with the other parents so they can spend the day with their kids." He took a knee. "Give Daddy big hugs."

Maribel hesitated, then ran to him and he caught her as she tripped on her last step, scooping her into his arms, kissing her forehead.

With any luck, he'd be done in time to tuck his precious little girl into bed. Losing her mother had not been easy on her last year, and part of the reason he desperately wanted to make his security consulting enterprise work was so that he could be around and she could grow up surrounded by people who loved her. Dylan couldn't bring back her mother, but he'd vowed their Bel would always know she'd been wanted and loved. Unlike Dylan, whose parents had dumped him with his grandmother at six months old because the responsibility of caring for a baby had proved too much for the free-spirited hipsters. They'd split up a year later and had rarely visited. No birthday cards. No high school graduation appearance. No showing at his daughter's christening.

Dylan's child would never know that brand of rejection.

She turned toward Rebecca and launched herself again.

"Hold on there." He caught her under her arms and pulled her back toward him. He helped secure her backpack before another round of hugs came.

Maribel stopped at the door and turned, smiling, one

hand holding on to Auntie Becca's, the other waving back at him. "Bye-bye, Da-da!"

"Have a good day at school. Learn everything you can."

"So I can be smarter than you," she squealed. Those adorable *r*'s rolling out like *w*'s. The pediatrician had assured him she'd sort it out in the next year or so. He knew he should work harder on pronunciation with her but it was so darn cute the way she said her words. Because he'd missed out on the first two years of her life, a selfish part of him didn't want her growing up any faster than she had to.

"That's right." Dylan watched Rebecca buckle Maribel into the spare car seat she'd pulled from her trunk. He stood at the window until the blue sedan disappeared down the drive.

His laptop was already booted up, so he snagged another cup of coffee and seated himself at the breakfast bar. No matter how hard he tried, he couldn't shake the feeling that Maribel needed a female influence in her life even if he couldn't imagine having time to find one. Relationships were complicated. They required communication and commitment. The only thing Dylan was devoted to at the moment was finishing his cup of coffee.

When he put his full attention to the case, it took about an hour of digging to find that Samantha had withdrawn five thousand dollars in cash from her bank four days ago. The withdrawal was timed perfectly to her disappearance. His trouble radar jumped up a few notches. She might've been forced to pull out the money, murdered and then dumped somewhere. No. Forget it. He couldn't allow himself to believe she'd been killed and that he'd be looking for a body. There were other possibilities. Maybe she'd decided to pack up and take a vacation. Everyone was burned out from recent events.

A quick call to her employer shot down that prospect. Samantha hadn't been to work in a week.

The probability foul play wasn't involved shrank by the nanosecond.

Dylan scanned online news outlets for crimes with unidentified females on the date she withdrew money.

He came up short and sighed with relief.

There were dozens of hospitals in Dallas, even more counting the suburbs. He narrowed his search down to a five-mile radius of where she lived and worked. The number shrank to five. He called each one looking for a Jane Doe, relieved when he didn't find her.

Next he reached out to the city morgue, which was not a call he wanted to make.

Relief flooded him at receiving the word that no Jane Does had been received in the past week.

Having exhausted obvious answers, he had to consider other possibilities. The first one that popped into his mind said she could be on the run. But from what?

This was Samantha he was thinking about. Nothing in her background suggested she had criminal inclinations. He'd known her personally for more than half his life. Wouldn't there have been signs along the way? Lies told here and there?

Of course, the tight-knit group of twelve-year-olds had disbanded after Shane's disappearance, but they'd all gone to the same high school, traveled in loosely the same circles. Didn't he know her?

She came from a large middle-class family, the youngest of four kids. Her dad had been in sales, so she'd moved around most of her young life. He'd cashed out their life savings and rented space on the town square to open a hardware store after her mother had died. Samantha had settled in Mason Ridge in fifth grade, just a year before the tragedy. She'd been a good student. She'd played volleyball at Mason Ridge High School well enough to earn a scholarship to a small university in Arkansas. And that had been when he'd lost touch with her.

Her brothers had spread out, going to different colleges and then settling in separate cities. Last Dylan had heard, they had families of their own. The trouble came with her mom's side. Several uncles had rap sheets longer than the menu at Chili's. But Samantha never spoke about them, and Dylan figured the family had cut ties long ago.

He tried her cell. The call went straight to voice mail.

The idea one of her distant relatives could've gotten her into trouble didn't sit well. No way would she get involved with them.

Dylan made a phone call to a technical-guru friend he'd used from time to time to hack into databases and phones. If a device had a firewall, Jorge could sneak past it unseen and get out with the same ability. He was the freakin' Houdini of hackers.

Jorge picked up on the second ring. Not surprising for a man who was at his computer 24/7. "What can I do you for?"

"I got a missing person. Need to find out who she was speaking to in the days surrounding her disappearance."

"Give me the details." His voice was all business.

Dylan relayed information like her phone number slowly into the receiver.

Jorge repeated the digits.

Dylan confirmed.

"Got it. Hold on a sec." The sound of fingers tapping across a keyboard came through the line.

"I can't get a location for you, but I can see who she's

been talking to. I see your number on here. You have a relationship with this girl?" Jorge asked.

"She's a friend."

"I heard about all that mess going on in your neck of the woods. Glad they caught the dude. Gives a whole new meaning to being burned, though." His jokes were crass but Dylan got it. While women sat down with glasses of wine and talked about emotions until they felt better, men joked. Dylan wasn't arguing one style over the other. It was just a guy's way of trying to get his arms around the stuff he didn't have a good handle on. "I'll send you an email with a list of the numbers, but there's something weird. She received several calls from a burn phone in the days prior to her vanishing act."

"None after?" Why would someone call her using a pay-as-you-go phone? Dylan didn't like any of this news. It took him down the path he didn't want to be true.

"Nope."

"What's the number?" Dylan searched for a pen and paper.

"I'll send it in the report. Won't do you any good calling it, though."

"Why's that?"

"The line's been disabled."

"Which means you can't trace it?"

"Nope. Did your friend get herself into some kind of trouble?"

"Looks like it," Dylan said. Several more scenarios ran through his mind. None he liked. He thanked Jorge and closed the call.

Dylan spent the rest of the morning tracking down Samantha's landlord in Dallas, who agreed to check out her place. Her car was gone from the parking garage of her condo. A few drawers had been left open in her bedroom, and her bathroom counter was empty. Experience had taught Dylan that women didn't go anywhere without their makeup bags.

Mail sat on the counter untouched. Other than a few necessary supplies, very little was missing from her condo. When she'd decided to take off, she hadn't brought much with her. A quick escape suggested someone on the run, just as he feared she might be. But again the question came up. Running from what? Or whom?

Was she dating someone? Dylan should've asked that question first. A woman's biggest threat in life was a man close to her—a boyfriend or spouse. Dylan's fists curled and released at the thought of any man hurting a woman. The notion hit him even harder now that he had a daughter. Let any guy try to hurt his Bel…

Anger roared through him like buckshot, exploding in every direction. He didn't need to go there about his child. Samantha deserved his focus.

The next trick would be to locate her. He kept his hunt inside Texas, figuring she'd stick with what she knew. Austin was her favorite city, or at least it used to be. He'd lost touch with her after high school. Taking a chance on his hunch, he decided to start his search in the live-music capital of the world, guessing she'd go somewhere familiar.

Once he narrowed the hunt there, finding her would be easy. Apartments had managers who followed rules, so an offer of cash to pay up a few months' rent would draw too much unwanted attention. She would most likely rent a house something near campus, so she could easily get around by throwing on a hoodie and shorts to blend in with students.

A quick internet search revealed there were 387 houses for rent in the city of Austin. Twenty-three when narrowed down to places on or near campus. Dylan put his resources to work finding out which ones had been pulled from the market the day Samantha disappeared. Two. With a fifty-fifty chance of success, Dylan gambled on the house nearest campus and checked the tenant. No dice. The place had been rented by four people. He hit the jackpot on the second.

He made a quick call to Ms. Anderson to let her know he had to leave town, and then located his duffel. The hope of being home by Maribel's bedtime fizzled as he stuffed a pair of jeans in the bag. He packed a sandwich to eat on the drive—roughly four hours one way, depending on traffic on I-35—left a note for Ms. Anderson to read *Goodnight Moon* to his daughter after tucking her into bed and locked the door behind him.

DYLAN LEANED AGAINST a tree six houses down from Samantha's. He'd driven his small sedan rather than his SUV in order to better navigate Austin traffic. Based on his research, a UT shuttle should be passing by in ten minutes to pick up college kids and deliver them to campus. With others hanging around waiting on transportation, he had a better chance of going unnoticed. With his six-foot-two-inch muscular frame, he looked as if he should be in athletic housing. Camo pants and the burned-orange UT shirt he'd bought at the gas station on the way into town should help camouflage him. Duffel slung over his shoulder, he did his best to blend in.

If Samantha was in trouble or being held hostage, he didn't want to tip off her captor. He had to consider the possibility that she wasn't acting on her own free will. Dylan planned to take nothing for granted.

His pulse kicked up a notch when she came into view, walking toward the front door of her rental alone. With a long and lean body like hers, she could easily be confused for a student athlete. Her high school years spent playing volleyball had paid off, especially with those legs.

He slipped on eyeglasses specially fitted with binocular lenses. Her smoky-brown hair cut in long shiny layers with bangs that skimmed along her brows brought out a deeply erotic shade of wide-set almond-shaped blue eyes. They stood out against her oval face. Samantha had always been beautiful. At least that much had stayed the same. She'd been smart, too. Her beauty had caught his attention. Her sharp wit and sense of humor had kept it. He hoped that she hadn't gone and done something stupid. Surely someone back home would've noticed if she'd changed.

Sometimes good girls were drawn to men who were bad for them. So far, there was no sign of a boyfriend. *Good.* He told himself it would be easier to help her with fewer people involved, and he didn't like the idea she'd be on the run with a man.

She glanced around, looking more nervous than afraid. Her long fluid layers of brown hair framed an almost too beautiful face and highlighted a graceful, swan-like neck.

Ignoring the rapid increase in his heartbeat at seeing her, he bowed his head and focused on the newspaper he held, pretending to be studying it as he kept her in his peripheral.

She unlocked the door, glanced left to right once more and then slipped inside.

Paranoid?

Dylan had half a mind to stomp over and demand to know what was going on. That would be a mistake. The simple fact was that he didn't know what he'd be walking into and didn't want to tip his hand. He slipped off the glasses and then slid them inside his duffel as the shuttle arrived. The crowd around him thinned, forming a line to get on the bus. He stood back, allowing others to crowd in front of him.

At the last second, he spun around, ducked his head and made a beeline toward her place. Moving around the side of the house, he crouched below the windows, careful to avoid being cut by overgrown holly bushes lining his path. He walked the perimeter, peeking inside windows through cracks in the closed blinds. From what he could tell so far, she was alone.

The back door was locked. It took all of three seconds to change that with his bump key. He slowly opened the door, moved inside the kitchen and listened. He already knew the layout of the house. Using the Department of Defense satellite, he'd homed in on the address and taken pictures of everything inside and out, to the level of detail of her furniture arrangement. Memorizing every inch of the space, every crevice, was a habit formed during his military days. There were two bedrooms and a kitchen in back, all of which had doors that led to a dining room. The master bedroom was off the living room. The place was set up like a maze.

Telltale clicks on a keyboard said she was on her laptop. The dining room was set up as a study room with tables pushed against the walls instead of a table and chairs.

Not risking chance, Dylan palmed his Glock, using it to lead the way.

"What are you doing here, Samantha?" He lowered his weapon when he was sure the place was clear.

Samantha jumped to her feet, the shock of seeing him evident on her face. It took her a moment before she was able to answer. "Me? I could ask you the same thing, Dylan." The accusation in Samantha's voice fired at him as though he stood in front of an execution squad. A mix of panic and fear crossed her features as she sat ramrod straight. Her gaze froze on his gun.

Her fearful expression tugged at his heart.

"I'm not going to hurt you." He surveyed the area. "Is there anyone else here?"

"Not that I know of." Her gaze darted to the front door and then back.

"What does that mean?"

"Did anyone follow you?" The suspicion in her eyes hit him harder than a shot of tequila for breakfast, with a similar burn in his chest.

"No."

"Are you sure?" More accusations fired in her tone.

"Yes." This wasn't the greeting he'd expected.

"How can I trust you?"

"You don't have to, sweetheart." He had no intention of hurting her. Her panicked expression ate at his insides. What was she so afraid of? Or maybe the better question was, what had she done?

He took another step toward her so he could really examine her. With her pallor, she looked as if she'd seen a ghost. "But it's me. And you know me."

"How did you find this place?" She didn't seem ready to concede anything.

"The internet. It wasn't hard," he said casually, trying to use his voice to calm her.

"If it was easy for you, then he can find me, too. I have to get out of here." Her pulse hammered at the base of her throat.

Finally, he was getting somewhere. Someone had her seriously spooked. Dylan shot her an apologetic look.

"Who are you involved with? A boyfriend?"

Her head was already shaking.

"Then, tell me who's looking for you and I can help."

She didn't respond. He needed to take another tack. Get her in the car for four hours, gain her trust and he'd get closer to finding the truth.

"I can see that you're in some kind of trouble. What are you running from?"

Her lips clamped shut.

"Everyone's worried. Come home with me and we'll sort this out," he offered, hoping he could appeal to her on a friendship level.

"No. It's too risky. He'll find me." That same frightened-animal look was in her eyes.

"Who will?"

"Thomas Kramer." She shivered involuntarily as she said his name.

"The Mason Ridge Abductor?" *Stunned* didn't begin to describe his reaction. No way. Dylan checked her pupils for signs of drugs, even though the Samantha he knew would never do such a thing. Something had her acting cagey. He saw pure, unadulterated fear in her gaze. "He's dead, sweetheart. A pile of ash. Remember? He can't hurt you from where he is."

She stood there, trembling, looking lost. *Damn.*

Dylan made a move to step forward, to comfort her. Her body stiffened, so he froze.

"It's not safe here. He'll find me."

"What are you talking about?" Dylan held his hands up in surrender, slowly, because he half feared she would bolt otherwise. "I'm moving to the couch to sit down so we can talk about this."

He walked deliberately.

She moved to the front window, peering outside through the slats in the blinds. "He might've followed you."

The look of panic on her face couldn't be faked. Something had her completely rattled, but Thomas Kramer was dead.

"Sit down beside me and tell me what happened," he said calmly.

"I have to get out of here." Her voice shook with fear and her eyes pleaded with him. She stalked back to the desk and reached inside a drawer.

"Stop right there." The last thing he needed was for her to do something desperate. Dylan ate the real estate between them in two quick strides and covered her hand, stopping her from raising it toward him. He ignored the fizz of attraction sizzling between them.

Her left fist was closed around an object. He turned her palm toward the ceiling, noticing her white-knuckle grip. "Open your hand slowly."

She did, exposing a fistful of cash.

"What's this for, Samantha?"

"Nothing. Take it and get out of here."

"You're trying to give me money to leave?"

"Whatever you want, take it. Just go."

"Rebecca sent me." If she wouldn't talk to him based on their history, maybe he could get through to her by using her friend's name.

"She shouldn't have," Samantha shot back. "This is no one's business but mine."

That didn't work. She seemed even more agitated. Maybe he could appeal to her softer side. "How can I help if you don't tell me what's going on?"

"I can't. I don't even know myself and it's too dangerous."

Dylan took a step away from her, releasing her hand, breaking contact before he revealed his body's reaction to her. Even then he felt the tension coiling inside his body. "Why not?"

"He'll kill me and everyone I love."

Chapter Two

"No one's going to hurt you, Samantha. And especially not a man who's already dead." Dylan fished his phone from his front pocket and then paused with his thumb hovering over Brody's number. "Your friends are worried. I need to call and let them know I found you."

She shook her head fervently. "He'll know. I don't know how but he'll figure it out if you do that. And then we'll all be in danger again."

"Does this have anything to do with the phone calls you received before you took off?" Dylan wouldn't rule out the possibility someone was using her fear of the Mason Ridge Abductor to manipulate her.

A look of shock crossed her features. She quickly recovered, smoothing her open hand down her jeans.

"I already told you." Her gaze darted around the room, no doubt looking for an escape route. "You don't believe me."

Frazzled, frightened, she had the disposition of a cornered animal. And since that rarely turned out well for the person who tried to capture it, Dylan put his hands up, keeping his cell in his hand, where she could see it. "Look, sweetheart, you're safe. I'm here. Tell me exactly what's going on so I can help you."

"I don't expect you to understand. But Thomas Kramer is coming." Eyes wild, she bolted for the door.

Thomas Kramer was dead. Someone was trying to manipulate her by using her fear of the past. Dylan dropped his phone and caught her as she reached the front door. Whatever she'd gotten herself into was clearly more than she could handle. He bear-hugged her from behind and pulled her far enough away from the door that the handle was out of reach.

She kicked and screamed, and her foot connected with his groin.

Doubled over, he tightened his grip around her mid-section as he took a few deep breaths to stave off blinding pain and nausea.

He'd almost felt sorry for her when she was stumbling over her words, trying to distract him so she could bolt. But experience had taught him innocent people didn't try to run.

"Be still," Dylan bit out curtly. His thick arms were like vise grips around her hips, and it was impossible not to notice the solid wall that was Dylan flush against her bottom. She couldn't blame him for his words coming out harshly after she'd kicked him in the groin.

If she could loosen his grip, she might be able to break free and run. No matter how much she wanted to confide in Dylan, she couldn't. The Mason Ridge Abductor had returned, attacked her in the parking lot of her office, and then her father had disappeared after confirming as much and telling her not to try to find him. He'd told her to hide and stay hidden until he could sort this mess out that had begun fifteen years ago. And even though Dylan didn't know it, she was saving him, too. He didn't need to get involved and she'd said too much already.

The door was so close. She stretched her fingers toward it. Too far.

Drawing from all her strength, she tensed her body and then jabbed her elbow into Dylan's midsection. If he could find her, so could Kramer, and her father had said the Mason Ridge Abductor would use her to force him out of hiding.

On some level, she knew Kramer was a pile of ashes, but someone could be using his name to hide behind.

Dylan coughed, ground out a few choice words and then spun her around to face him. His fingers gripped the flesh on her shoulders tightly.

She couldn't budge. He'd made sure of it.

"Make another move and I'll ensure you regret it." He'd bent down to her level. Penetrating clear green eyes glared at her.

This close, his face was all sharp angles and hard planes, with a severe jawline on a squared jaw, intelligent eyes. *Good-looking* didn't begin to describe his features. He wasn't a pretty boy. No, this poster child for strength and general level red-hotness had the rugged looks that came with knowing how to take care of himself. His tightly clipped sandy-brown hair reminded her he was ex-military. No way could she get away from him going toe to toe, even if she was close to his height at six foot. Growing up with three older brothers had taught her a thing or two about her own limitations.

"You're hurting me," she angled, hoping he'd slacken his grip enough for her to escape.

"I'm sorry about that. I loosen my hold and you'll run for it. I need you right here. It's me, Samantha. I've said this before but it's worth repeating. You can talk to me."

"Fine. Let me go and I promise not to do anything stupid." Even if he was determined to get himself involved, she couldn't allow it.

"And I'm supposed to believe you based on what? Your word?"

"Yes. You are." Looking into those green eyes, seeing she wasn't getting anywhere, Samantha decided to take another tack. If he was going to believe her, she'd have to tell him something concrete. And yet he wouldn't believe her if she did. She could hardly believe it. "Look, I know how crazy this sounds, but Kramer is either reaching out from the grave or someone is pretending to be him."

He shot her a look that had her wondering if he thought she was crazy. She hadn't thought about how all this might look to an outsider until then. There was a hint of curiosity in his eyes, too.

"You have my word that I won't try to run away from you, Dylan. Now let me go." She jerked her shoulders, surprised when he loosened his grip.

"Tell me something, Samantha. Because right now you look guilty of something bad, something that has you on the run, and if I didn't know you better, I'd be calling the cops." As if for emphasis, he picked up his phone.

"No cops. Promise me." She rubbed her shoulders to bring blood back to them, trying to figure out what she could say that wouldn't implicate her father. She wanted to trust Dylan, but she couldn't risk it. If he knew, he wouldn't walk away. He wasn't the type.

"Sorry if I hurt you." He motioned toward the couch. "Sit."

"I'm fine."

Sharp green eyes stared at her. He'd been wild when they were young, and there was more than a hint of that same feral tendency in his features now. "We can do this one of two ways. You sit willingly. Or I tie you up until you tell me the truth. Your choice."

She moved to the couch and plopped down. Anger boiled inside her. Everyone thought that the Mason Ridge Abductor was gone, but he wasn't. And he was coming after her. He'd surprised her, then called and threatened her if she didn't meet him after she got away.

Dylan glanced out the front window and then focused those intense greens on her. Eye contact wasn't the best idea, because when he looked at her, her stomach flipped. Dylan was easy to look at. She wouldn't deny an attraction sizzled under the surface, one that had been simmering since before high school. Even with his bad-boy reputation, she'd always known there was something good about him deep inside.

"I was careful not to leave a trail." The blood was finally returning to her shoulders. Bruising would be the least of her problems.

"Your lack of a path helped narrow the scarch. You were somewhere within driving distance because you used your car. I also knew you'd want an internet connection. Austin's your favorite city, so I took a chance. From there, all I had to do was figure out which house you'd rented."

She'd been that transparent? So much for thinking she could hide. Frustration burned through her. Too bad she didn't have the criminal tendencies of her mother's side of the family.

"I'm truly sorry about earlier. You know I would never hurt you on purpose," he said.

She did know. Dylan was a good guy.

"I'm going to ask you again. What's going on?" His brow arched and he was examining her face as if her head was about to start spinning.

Could she risk telling Dylan anything else? He already looked ready to strap her into the first straitjacket he could find. And what if she told Dylan what she feared? That her father was somehow involved or at least covering for someone else that night Rebecca and Shane had gone missing fifteen years ago? Or that if she shared what she feared, Dylan would be in this as deeply as she was?

The crackle of a branch breaking sent both of them to the front window.

"Don't let anyone see you." Dylan pulled her down, his strong hands firmly on her hips.

In the street, the screech of tires sent her adrenaline into overdrive. "We can't stay here."

Dylan opened the curtain in the front window and cursed. "I can't help you if I don't know what you've gotten yourself into. You haven't given me anything to work with yet."

"I don't know who I can trust anymore. All I know is this whole thing is bigger than we originally thought." Kramer was believed to have acted alone. What if he hadn't? What if others had been involved in the crime or the cover-up?

"What 'thing,' Samantha? What are you talking about?" He stared at her for a long moment.

Could she tell him? She wanted to talk to someone. The past four days had been terrifying alone. She shook her head.

"This is a college town. There are people everywhere, so the noise outside might be nothing." Dylan's voice came out in a whisper as he surveyed the area through the windows.

She had to admit, having Dylan with her steadied her fried nerves. "Do you really think I'm crazy? Or involved in something illegal?"

"No. But I've never seen you this scared." Dylan held out his hand. "Come back to Mason Ridge with me and we'll sort this out."

"I can't go home." She didn't take it.

"You can stay at my house." His expression had her thinking he believed she needed to be locked up in one of those high-priced sanctuaries by the ocean rather than his place, but to his credit, he didn't say it.

Even so, she dared to allow a small bubble of hope to expand, the first since this nightmare had begun a week ago.

Another crunch noise came from just outside the glass.

"Stay down." His gaze ping-ponged from her to the window as he tightened his grip on the handle of his gun. His movements were assured, graceful.

Even with him there, Samantha couldn't relax. Not when a man could reach out from the grave, as Kramer had. What if the guy really was dead and all logic said he was? What if someone else was involved? How big could this thing be?

The little bubble of hope burst. Despair pressed heavy on her chest.

"Several men are headed this way." The concern in his voice was enough to fry what was left of her nerves. "What aren't you telling me?"

"I told you everything."

"I asked this before and I'm going to ask it again. Are you involved in something illegal?"

"No."

"Drugs?"

"That would be illegal."

"Is someone forcing you to do something you don't want to? Are they coming?"

"It's not like that."

Dylan scooped his cell off the floor next to her. "Obviously, there's something else at work here. I don't like this one bit."

With him on her side, she might have a chance of fighting back. Grabbing money from her account and disappearing had been a knee-jerk reaction. She could see how that might make her look guilty of a crime.

"You need to get away from me before anyone sees you." Samantha hated the panic in her voice—the panic that had been beating in her chest like a drum since this ordeal had begun. The person claiming to be Kramer had been clear. Involve anyone else and he'd hurt them and everyone they loved.

"Do you trust me?"

She looked into his sharp green eyes. God help her, but she did. Of course, there weren't a lot of options at the moment. "Yes."

"Then, let's get out of here." He tucked his cell in his duffel.

"How do you plan to do that?" she asked.

The crack of a bullet split the air.

Chapter Three

Before Samantha had time to argue, Dylan had her on the floor. He needed to find cover in order to put mass between the two of them and the shotgun blasts firing toward them. He urged Samantha forward, crawling on hands and knees toward the kitchen. The feel of a body like hers underneath him, especially the way hers fit his, gave him a thrill of sexual excitement, but right now he didn't need his body reacting inappropriately. Nor did he need the distraction.

The three-foot crawl space between the fridge and the wall in the kitchen would offer some shield. Guiding her there, he followed. "Do everything I say."

Her cobalt-blue eyes were wide when she nodded.

Time to move.

Dylan shouldered his duffel and entwined Samantha's fingers in his, ignoring the pulse of electricity vibrating up his arm. His vehicle was parked two streets over. If they could make it out of the back of the house, circle around and cut across the street, they had a chance to break free.

He carefully zigzagged through the bushes along the path, hoping like hell they didn't run into whoever was shooting at them. With any luck, the shooter would be inside the house by now.

The glint of metal shone between houses directly across the street. That was what he got for wishing.

Dylan squinted against the bright sun, tucked Samantha behind him and ran like hell, darting side to side as he crossed the street.

Halfway across, a bullet struck the center of his chest, knocking the wind out of him. The impact, equivalent to being hit with a rubber mallet, knocked him back. He stumbled a few steps before falling on his backside and then scrambling behind a car so he could catch his breath. The Kevlar he wore kept the slug from piercing his chest.

Samantha's scream made the hair on his neck stand up. She obviously thought he'd been shot. And he had been. But it was okay.

She dropped down next to him.

There was no time to explain, so he gripped her hand tighter. Dylan dragged in a few breaths, and then pushed on, hoping the shooter hadn't readjusted, ready to fire another round.

Dylan guided them in between the buildings.

Forging ahead, he cleared another block and palmed his keys. His vehicle was in sight when he disarmed the alarm and unlocked the doors remotely.

If he could get the pair of them out of there, they had a chance at escape.

Dylan let go of Samantha's hand in time for her to dash around to the passenger side and get in. She sat there, stunned.

Out in the open like this, they were extremely vulnerable to attack.

Key ready, Dylan fired up the engine and peeled out of there.

"You're going to be fine."

"They shot you." The disbelief in Samantha's voice

indicated she hadn't had time to process everything that had just happened. It was a lot for a civilian to take in, and she was doing better than expected.

"I'm good. See." Dylan used his right hand to pull up his shirt enough for her to see his thin Kevlar vest. His left gripped the steering wheel as he wound through the residential area and away from the shrieking sirens. His focus had to be on the road as he assessed everyone they passed for potential threat. "I'll end up with a nasty bruise. That's all."

"Okay." That one word was spoken soft and small, almost without air. Her vulnerability pierced a different set of his armor.

He dropped his shirt and returned his hand to the steering wheel, checking the rearview to see if they had any company. So far, so good. One wrong turn and the story could change drastically. "We need to find the closest police station."

"No, please. He'll find my father if I involve the law." The desperation in her voice had him thinking twice.

"Samantha, we were just shot at. You're scared beyond belief. I believe you when you say you aren't involved in anything illegal. So let's go to the police and get protection."

"As soon as this car slows, I'll jump out. You shouldn't be part of this." She gripped the door handle. "Promise you won't go to the cops."

"Tell me why not." That was the second time she'd specifically insisted he shouldn't be involved. What the hell was that all about?

"I already did. He's going to kill my father."

"Who is?"

"Thomas Kramer, the Mason Ridge Abductor."

"He's dead, Samantha. He can't hurt you."

"You asked about the phone calls before." Her voice sounded resigned.

"And?"

"I was walking home from work last Tuesday. It was late. I stayed to finish up a project and was the last one to leave the office. Someone jumped me. I was shocked, scared, but I fought. I somehow managed to get away."

"Did you report it?"

"Of course. The police said it was most likely an attempted robbery. At first I thought the whole incident was random, too. When I told my father, he started freaking out. Made me promise not to leave my condo. Begged me not to get the police or anyone else involved. Said he'd make everything right. Told me to give him a little time and that he'd done a bad thing. I didn't know what to think or do. I panicked. Took a few vacation days and didn't leave my condo. Then the phone calls started. Someone saying he was the real Thomas Kramer said he wanted to meet. Said he had something of mine. He said if I involved the police, he'd kill me and my father. I stopped answering. When a stranger knocked on my door, I panicked again. I gathered a few of my things, waited for the guy to leave and then took off."

"Sounds as if someone is hiding behind Kramer's name. There's a cell phone in my duffel. I need you to take it out," he said.

"Please, no. Don't call the police."

"I won't. Not until we figure this out."

"Not 'we.' I need to lie low until I find a way to reach my father."

"I'm not going anywhere, Samantha."

"You can't be here."

"Why not? Whoever is doing this can't hurt you or me. We'll get to the bottom of it. I'm not leaving until we figure this out. I need to make a call to arrange a place for us to stay. Will you get me the phone?"

She blew out a sharp breath but didn't immediately move.

"I'm your only chance, Samantha. You need to decide."

"Okay. Fine. Where is it? Here?" She pointed to one of four zippers on the front of the pack.

"Inside the main compartment." He didn't take his eyes off the road. She'd find other things in there, too. Another gun. A hand grenade. Things she could use against him if she completely freaked.

"I found it." Her delicate skin had gone pale. She looked exhausted.

"Look in the contacts for Brody."

"Got him."

A helicopter flew overhead.

Dylan glanced over at Samantha in time to see her hand shaking.

She drew in a breath.

"Call Brody and put this on speaker." Dylan searched his rearview. So far, no one had followed them. He banked a U-turn.

"Where are we going?" she asked.

"Not on I-35. Whoever that was will be expecting that. And we don't know how many people are involved."

"Won't he scour the city until he finds us?"

"He'll try."

Brody answered on the first ring. "What's going on?"

"You're on speaker and I have Samantha in the car."

"Is she okay?"

"Yes."

"Rebecca will be so relieved. She's been worried sick. You guys heading home?" Brody asked.

"Can't."

"Why not?"

"Long story, but we need your help." He didn't want to repeat everything that Samantha had told him. It would only dredge up bad memories for Rebecca, especially since this couldn't be Thomas Kramer. Thomas Kramer had acted alone. And Thomas Kramer was dead. Not to mention the fact that he was part of the breakdown crew for a traveling festival. Not exactly someone who had the connections or money to hire men like the ones who'd come after Samantha. The only person in town who could financially back an operation like this would be someone like Charles Alcorn, the town's wealthiest resident. But it couldn't be him.

Alcorn had played a critical role in the investigation fifteen years ago. Everyone in town had been thoroughly investigated. Dylan was getting punchy.

It could, however, be someone tied to Kramer.

Whatever game this creep was playing was about to end.

"What do you need from me?" Brody asked.

"Get me what you can on Thomas Kramer. I want to know everything about him. Friends, family, known hangouts."

"You got it." Brody cursed under his breath.

"Why him?"

"I'll explain later." Dylan cut a hard right and then a left. "But we need a safe place to stay."

"Why not go to the police?" Having served in the military, Brody still had connections—connections that could come in handy.

"Not yet."

"I'll make a few calls and find a place for you to hide within the hour. I have a lot of friends in Austin. Until then, stay on the move. We'll figure this out," Brody said. "I'll let the others know what's going on, too."

Dylan looped around downtown four times before the phone rang again.

"I have a location for you. I found a small place behind a bar on Sixth Street." Brody relayed the address. "I would've liked to get you farther out of town but I figured you'd want internet access and you needed someplace quick. Plus, with all the foot traffic, it'll be easier to disappear in the crowd. Big Mike is working the bar and he's expecting you both. He'll have keys and can give you any passwords you need to use the internet."

"Hey, thanks, Brody."

"Keep me posted. And good luck."

Luck? He blew out a sharp breath. Since he'd left his four-leaf clover in his other pants, he'd have to rely on skills the US Army had taught him to stay alive.

SAMANTHA WAS BEGINNING to shake off the mental fog that came with the hard slap of reality that she was now on the run with Dylan. She shouldn't notice his thick, muscled arms. Nor should she get too comfortable in the sense of relief being this near him brought.

If she was going to be running for her life, she certainly wanted to be with a man who looked as if he could handle whatever was thrown at them. That was a given. But feeling as though somehow everything was magically going to be all right because Dylan had shown up was naive, no matter how capable he was. And her father was still in danger. "What's the plan now?"

"You tell me everything. We put our heads together and figure this out."

"I already said. He's going to keep coming until both my father and I are dead. Dad said as much." She rubbed her temples to stave off the headache threatening. It was a potent mix of frustration and exhaustion.

"Then, we need to write another ending." He touched her hand to reassure her but instead it sent fissures of heat swirling up her arm.

"We can't hide forever. Whoever is behind this will find us." She hated how weak and fearful her own voice sounded. But she was afraid. And there was no use hiding it.

Dylan's gaze shifted from the rearview to the road as he jerked the steering wheel in another hard right turn. "We have company."

Horns blared as Dylan made a few quick turns, navigating the crowded streets of downtown. Samantha's "fight, freeze or flight" response rocketed through the roof and she battled against the urge to jump out of the car and set out on foot.

Traffic was so thick the black sedan couldn't get close. Yet it kept pace with every turn six cars back.

Dylan muttered a curse at the same time Samantha thought it. With Dylan involved, she feared the threats against her, her family and her friends were going to be delivered on.

"I'm scared." She hated admitting it, but acknowledging her feelings had always made them less overwhelming. Especially after her mother's death.

"Think of what you'll be doing next week."

"What?" Damn weakness. Growing up in a house full of boys had taught her to fend for herself. Yet she was so out of her league here that her nerves were spiraling out of control. She needed to calm down and figure this out. Everything had happened so fast she hadn't had a chance to process it.

"You know what I'll be doing?" he said, his calm voice settling over her.

She shook her head.

"I'll be picking Maribel up from school about now."

The image of him, all muscle-and-steel man, tenderly holding his little girl, stirred her heart in ways she'd never experienced. She'd seen him at the grocery with Maribel a few times, witnessed his tenderness with his daughter.

"You need to drop me off somewhere and go to her."

"I'm not leaving you alone, Samantha. End of conversation." A mix of emotion played out across his features, determination rising to the top. "What about you? What are you going to be doing this time next week?"

"My dad invited me to go fishing with him." Her dad. Where was he? *What have you done, Daddy?*

"Good. Focus on that when you get scared. Know that you will be sitting next to him on his boat, hauling in the largest catfish either of you have ever seen."

"That's his favorite. Loves the taste of blues."

"The man has good taste."

Samantha had a clear mental picture, and it was working.

"Better?"

"Yes." Much to her surprise, it was helping a little. Then again, Dylan's confidence was addicting. She'd have to work harder to ignore the sensual shivers his touch brought.

"Hand me the duffel." His voice was level and calm, the complete opposite of the emotions still trilling through Samantha.

"Okay. What now? What do we do?" The sheer amount of foot traffic on the sidewalk and the streets made it impossible to get away. If they didn't make a move soon, the driver would edge his way closer until he could get a good shot.

Dylan told her the address of the hideout.

"On three, I want you to open that door and run into the alley. Don't look back. No matter what happens, keep going. Got it?"

"What if—?"

"One…"

The thought of splitting up and going in different directions had Samantha bracing for a full-on panic attack. She'd have to trust that Dylan knew what he was doing.

Given what she'd been through in the past few days, the idea of trusting anyone was almost laughable.

"Two…"

He glanced at her as though searching for confirmation.

She nodded and gripped the door handle.

"Three. Go!"

She pushed the door open and burst from the car, jolting toward the alley lined with parked vehicles until her thighs burned. Students were everywhere.

Dodging in and out of the human obstacle course, she ran harder as panic mounted. An icy grip around her rib cage squeezed. Where was Dylan?

She couldn't even think of anything happening to him. His little girl needed him.

The sound of shots fired made her knees wobble and the crowds scatter. She steadied herself and charged ahead, fighting the urge to look back, knowing that losing a precious second of advantage could cost her her life.

Where was he?

The absence of those intense green eyes on her was like being thrust into darkness. She'd do almost anything to see him again, to know he was okay. The only reason she missed him was because she hurt for his little girl, she tried to convince herself. Samantha knew what it was like to lose a parent. It had nothing to do with the fact that he'd become her lifeline in a matter of hours. Everything about his presence was soothing.

He'd risked his life to save her and she hadn't had a chance to thank him yet.

The thought of doing any of this without him brought on deep physical pain. She told herself it was because of his professional skills and not because of his strength or virility.

Except he had Maribel. And what if something happened to him?

Samantha would never forgive herself.

Dylan parked the car and ran. He'd given Samantha a three-minute head start. He ducked, narrowly avoiding the bullet that lodged into the brick two feet from his head. As far as good days went, barely escaping a head shot didn't rack up as one of them. With so many innocent civilians around, he wouldn't return fire and risk a stray bullet.

Zigzagging in and out of buildings, he cut left.

Samantha had no phone or GPS to guide her. She'd have to rely on the instructions he'd given her. Since she was in an understandably stressed-out state, he couldn't count on that happening.

Risking a glance behind, he caught sight of two men following him. Neither broke off in Samantha's direction. That was a win. Now all he had to do was shake them. Her theory of this being carried out by Thomas Kramer disintegrated. He'd worked alone, and whoever was behind this had resources.

Dylan pushed his legs harder, faster. The guys behind him were already showing signs of fatigue.

Good.

As long as he kept his pace, he could outrun them. Ducking in between houses, he circled back. Samantha should be long gone, but if she was in trouble, he hoped he'd get there in time.

The *whop-whop-whop* of a chopper sounded overhead; no doubt shots being fired had drawn police attention. He slid underneath a Suburban and waited.

After sixty seconds, the chopper noise faded.

Glancing around, he noted that the coast seemed clear of foot traffic, too.

As he slid out from underneath the SUV, a blow to the head came out of nowhere. Dylan stumbled forward, checking his balance by grabbing the SUV. Without turning, he dropped to a squat and, with one leg extended, swept behind him.

The contact was followed by a *clunk*, confirming a direct hit.

Pivoting, Dylan covered the guy who'd hit him with a quick jab and then ran. He needed to locate Samantha. He could only pray that his diversion tactic had worked. He'd promised to protect her. The thought of her being vulnerable was a sucker punch to his gut. He told himself it was because she was counting on him and he didn't want to let her down, and that it had nothing to do with the electricity humming inside him when she was near.

He blocked the image of her lying in the alley somewhere, hurt, out of his mind.

Focusing on their next steps, he decided his first action would be to change their appearances. The hideout would most likely have a much-needed change of clothes. He hoped she'd be there. Dylan covered the few blocks quickly.

The key was with Big Mike, just as Brody had said.

"I let in a lady several minutes ago," Big Mike said. "Said her name was Samantha. She looked scared of her own shadow."

After a heartfelt handshake and a thank-you, Dylan headed around back and climbed up the wooden staircase.

He slipped through the back door and waited.

"Samantha," he whispered. There was no sound of her. With DEFCON silence, he crept through the small apartment. The living room and kitchen were clear. He moved to the bedroom next, careful not to make a noise. If she was there, she wasn't giving away her position. Why did that make his chest swell with pride?

He pushed the thought out of his mind, reminding himself that women were good at hiding things when they wanted to be. All things done in darkness eventually came to light. What else was Samantha keeping from him?

Out of his peripheral vision, he saw movement to his left inside the closet. A curtain acted as a makeshift door.

Caution dictated that he make no assumptions. The person was most likely Samantha, but until he had a visual, he wouldn't take it for granted. There was always the possibility that someone had gotten to her.

Damn.

Dylan took a step back.

The curtain burst open and Samantha sprang toward him. She landed with her body flush with his, and he tried not to think about how long it had been since a woman had been in his arms.

"Dylan. Thank God it's you." Shock was in her eyes

and deeply written across the lines of her forehead. "I was so scared."

"Of course it is," he soothed.

She gulped in air and he could see her pulse racing wildly.

"I'm here now. Everything's okay," he said, holding her.

"They were so close and I heard the shot. Oh, God, I panicked." She gulped another breath like a fish struggling out of water. "I—I—I didn't know what to do, so I ran here as fast as I could."

Another swallow of air.

She was about to hyperventilate.

Dylan could either slap her or kiss her to snap her back to reality. Since he'd never once lifted a hand to a woman and had no plans to start now, the choice was clear. He dipped his head low and pressed his lips against hers, half expecting another knee to his groin in return.

Shock registered when her lips moved against his and her fingers tunneled into his hair, deepening the kiss.

She pulled away first, pushing him back a step and glaring at him. "We need to figure this out."

He threw his hands up in surrender. "I was just trying to calm you down. I'm here as your friend."

It was a kiss he wouldn't forget anytime soon but a line that should never have been crossed, no matter how many times he'd wanted to do that in high school. *Since high school.*

"You'd do well to remember that." Her breathing had steadied, but she was angry. "We need a different plan. I can go to one of my brothers' places. You can't be involved."

"I'm sorry for what I did just now, but I still want to help."

Her head was already shaking. "Not a good idea. He was specific. I should've just gone to my brothers in the first place and not tried to figure this out on my own. Then, you wouldn't be here."

Dylan figured he'd led this guy straight to her. What happened earlier was on him. His ringtone broke through the awkward moment. He immediately answered when he saw Brody's name, noticing that he had a missed call.

"There's no good way to put this," Brody started, and an ominous feeling rolled through Dylan.

"Just come out with it." This wasn't going to be good. Waiting never made it better.

A deep sigh came across the line. "I wanted to notify you before the Amber Alert was issued. Maribel is missing."

Chapter Four

Dylan dropped to his knees. A dozen emotions pinged through his chest, rapid-fire like an AR-15 and with the same devastating effects. Rage battled to the surface, making him want to rip apart the first thing he could get his hands on. Ten years ago—hell, three—and he would've done just that. He was a different man now, and especially since Maribel had come into his life.

The image of his little girl waving to him at the kitchen door wearing the Mickey Mouse backpack that was almost as big as she was assaulted him. His military training kicked in, and that was the only reason he didn't explode in anger. It was the only thing keeping him from putting his fist through the nearest wall.

"Tell me exactly how it happened," he said through clenched teeth.

"First of all, Mrs. Applebee tried to call. She didn't want to lose time, so she immediately phoned me when she couldn't reach you or Ms. Anderson." Ms. Anderson was first on the emergency call list. Brody and Rebecca were second.

"Maribel was on the playground at the Dinosaur Park," Brody continued, "and teachers were stationed at each corner. Mrs. Applebee blew the whistle. Kids lined up.

Teachers counted heads. They turned up one short." Brody's voice was racked with agony.

Dylan knew his friends loved Maribel, too. That wasn't the thought he intended to focus on at the moment, and yet his brain didn't want to accept the reality that she was missing.

This had to be a mistake.

"Any chance she's inside somewhere? Hiding in one of the bathrooms at the ranger station?" he asked.

"The headmaster checked each one personally. She and the staff looked in every possible nook and cranny. Mrs. Applebee called the sheriff to file a report immediately."

Dylan was four hours away in Austin while his daughter was probably scared half to death wandering around somewhere, lost. He didn't even want to go there with the possibility she could be lost in the woods overnight. What kind of father was he to let this happen?

He pushed to his feet.

"We're all searching for her. We'll get her back. Stay positive, bro," Brody said. His solemn tone belied his words. "This is not your fault."

Yes, it is. Guilt raided Dylan. He was supposed to be on that field trip. If he'd kept his schedule as planned, then Maribel would be safe right now and not out there alone, stranded, scared.

It wasn't like his daughter to wander off.

Maybe Lyndsey had had good reason to be afraid that Dylan would be a lousy parent. She'd never really told him why she'd kept their daughter from him.

Samantha took Dylan's fisted hand, opened it and, palm to palm, wrapped her fingers around his. He squeezed hers and then let go. He walked across the room, turned toward the door and spoke low into his cell. "Have you spoken to the sheriff?"

"Rebecca is trying to get through to him now. She's been getting the runaround." Brody paused a beat. "She's sick about this. Said it's all her fault for asking you for a favor."

"She couldn't have known this would happen." The hope that this could be a mistake drained out of Dylan like water out of a tub. The harsh reality set in that his baby girl was missing.

"We're going to find her," Brody reassured him. "No matter what it takes."

The air thinned as if it had been sucked out of the room. The notion that Dylan might not ever see his Bel again pressed down on his chest with the force of a drill.

"We'll find her. And we'll bring her home," Brody said.

"I'm coming."

"It's not safe for you on the highway. Whoever's after Samantha will be waiting."

"Yeah? They're about to get a surprise." Dylan searched for his duffel. He'd blow up the whole freakin' town of Austin if it meant getting to Mason Ridge faster.

Samantha sank to the floor. "He took her. He said if anyone helped me they'd regret it."

All thoughts of his daughter wandering off on her own exploded in an audible crack.

This was a coordinated attack, bringing up the question once again of who would have resources to pull something like this off.

Dylan dropped the phone, turned to face Samantha and then stalked toward her. "What else do you know?"

She gasped. Tears streaming down her cheeks did

nothing to soften the steel fury coursing through him, making his veins burn.

"I already told you everything."

"You better start talking or I'll walk you outside and dump you on the street myself. We'll see how long it takes for those men to find you." He wouldn't do it, but she didn't know that and he needed to know exactly what she knew. Rather than allow his violent side to take over, he paced.

She looked up at him. The fear in her eyes didn't sit well with him, but he didn't have it in him right now to go easy on her, not while his baby was out there somewhere, God knew where, with people who wanted to use her to get to Samantha.

Her eyes were glossy and wide, fearful. They had an almost animallike quality to them. "He must know you're involved. That's why I didn't want you here in the first place. You should've just let me deal with this on my own."

"I couldn't leave you alone, Samantha." She had tried to push him away and get him out of there from the second he'd shown up.

"Thomas Kramer or whoever is behind this didn't hurt the boys. We have to hold on to the hope that he won't change that now," she reasoned.

"We have a small army after us." Dylan didn't voice his fear that he'd led them straight to her. Someone must've been watching the movements of the group of her friends to see if anyone came to find her. But why? Who else was involved? "My daughter is missing."

The US Army–trained sniper inside him—the man who could set aside personal feelings and regard for life in order to fire at a target—wanted to force more information out of her. But the man, the father he'd become knew that would just shock her deeper into her shell. He sank down in front of her. Desperation was as unforgiving as the bare wood floor against his knees. "I've got nothing here. I need your help."

Looking into Dylan's intelligent and intense green eyes stripped away Samantha's defenses. She saw that same look that had been in her eyes when she'd learned about her mother's accident. That had been Samantha's fault, too. Guilt pressed down on her shoulders until her arms grew numb. Her mother had been making a school run during a snowstorm. Samantha had forgotten her math folder. Some of the roads had been icy. Trotter Road had been the fastest route to school but it had that long bridge.

Her mother's car had broken through the ice. A chill raced down Samantha's spine at the memory.

And now a little girl's life was on the line…

Telling anyone about her father might put him in more danger. And yet *not* doing everything she could to help made her feel as if she was acting right along with the bad guys—an accomplice to the kidnapping. Her father had done something. She'd known instantly when she'd heard his voice on the phone last week. He was far from a perfect man, but he was a good person deep down. And he wouldn't want an innocent little girl trapped in the middle of this horrific mess.

Forgive me, Daddy.

"I'll tell you everything I know," she said, with the caveat that it wasn't much.

She took a deep breath to fortify herself and then told him every detail she could remember about the attack, the stalker and her father's words that he'd fix this one more time.

"When was the last time you spoke to your father?" Dylan asked.

"Less than a week ago. Right before I left town. He said he needed time to sort this out and that I should be careful. I wanted to see him but he refused. Said it was too dangerous to say where he was. At first I thought maybe he would go to one of my brothers' places. I called around the next day but none of them knew where he might be. They asked if they should be worried and I told them no. They have enough on their plates already and I really didn't know what else to tell them. Plus, I just thought, what could my dad have done? He's a nice guy. Pays his taxes ahead of schedule. Tends to the shop. He gave up drinking years ago, so it couldn't be related to that."

"How's the business doing? Any chance he owes someone he shouldn't?"

"It seems to be doing well."

"Desperate people can be very good at hiding things."

She knew firsthand the truth in those words. When her father was drinking, he'd come up with all kinds of sneaky ways to cover his tracks. "I got nothing. I mean, the business is good. I'd have to take a closer look at the books to be certain. He didn't do well when Mom died but we became his life after he stopped drinking." Samantha's voice still hitched when she talked about her mother, the pain still raw after all these years.

"What are we missing?" Dylan sat back on his heels and rubbed his temples. "We need to figure out a way to get back to Mason Ridge."

"Do that and we might be playing right into this guy's hands."

"I can't sit here and do nothing." The intensity to his voice didn't ease.

"Yeah, well, go outside and we might make it worse."

"That's impossible," he ground out. "My little girl is missing and I was supposed to be the one volunteering on the field trip. Me. I should've been there instead of running off for a case. This is my fault and she's probably scared to death. She already lost her mother and now she's alone again."

"You're a good father," she said, trying to soothe him.

"Really? How so? Do most fathers allow their children to be kidnapped?" he snapped.

"You didn't know this would happen. And you wouldn't be here if you had. If anyone's to blame, it's me. This is my fault, not yours." A heavy weight pressed on her chest. It was because of Samantha that her mother was gone. And now a little girl was in danger. How could that not feel like her fault, too?

Why hadn't Dylan listened to her before?

He was right, though. This couldn't possibly be the work of one man.

She crossed her arms over her chest. "We can't change what has already happened. All we can do is find my father and find out who is really behind this. Together."

"Like hell you're coming with me. You're in enough jeopardy as it is."

"What do you plan to do alone?" Dylan was already gathering his things and searching for what she figured had to be keys.

"Find my daughter and bring her home safely."

"How do you figure you'll accomplish that?"

"By talking to your father." He located his cell and then thrust it toward her. "Get him on the phone."

"He won't pick up."

"Then, leave a message. Tell him to call you back at this number."

"And what if whoever is responsible for all this is listening?" She waved her arms. "Do you really want them to have your cell? Can't they track you or something? Watch your movements? That doesn't seem like the smartest idea."

"That why you ditched yours?"

"Yes."

"Smart." It shouldn't have mattered that there was a hint of pride in that word. Maybe a hint of forgiveness, too?

"They won't trace mine," he said.

"How is yours different?"

"I have a friend who helps me out with technology. He scrambles the number for me when necessary, and he programmed in some kind of advanced encryption to make sure no one can keep an eye on me."

She cocked an eyebrow.

"With my security consulting business, I don't take chances." He disappeared into the other room and came back holding a pen and paper in his hand. He scribbled down digits. "Give your father this number."

Samantha took the offerings. She called her father, praying he would pick up. There'd been complete silence between them since he'd told her to hide, and it raised the hairs on the back of her neck thinking about it. Had they gotten to him? A shiver ran through her.

No, please. He was old. Whatever he'd done in his past couldn't have been that bad. Sure, he'd gone through a difficult phase after her mother had died. Everyone in the Turner household had, especially Samantha. His drinking had nearly done the family in. Then came that summer when Rebecca and Shane had been kidnapped. And Samantha's father had sobered up. He'd said it was the wake-up call he'd needed. That he couldn't stand to lose anyone else. He'd checked himself into rehab while her brothers took over the hardware shop. They'd stepped in to cover at home, too, and all had pitched in with household chores.

Hold on a minute. Samantha had met up with Rebecca recently at a restaurant in town. She'd brought her father along and he'd acted strangely around Rebecca. Samantha had been confused by his actions at first, but now they made sense. Had he been uncomfortable around her friend because he'd held back information about her and her brother's abduction?

The line rang but her father didn't answer.

Where was he?

If the person responsible for this craziness had gotten to him, then they most likely wouldn't still be looking for her. Right?

Why would they be after her at all?

There was only one logical explanation. They must think she knew what had really happened.

As expected, her father's line rolled into voice mail. She bit back a curse.

"Dad, please, I'm in trouble. I need to talk to you *now*. Call me back at this number." She rattled off the digits and ended the call.

Dylan paced as she stared at the phone, willing it to ring. *Come on, Daddy. Be okay. Call me back.*

She hadn't realized her hands were shaking until then.

This whole situation sounded all her internal warning bells. She'd known this guy had meant business from the start.

Regret engulfed her.

Dylan shouldn't be there. He shouldn't be involved. His daughter shouldn't be scared and alone right now because of Samantha.

"Get up," Dylan said harshly.

"What for?"

"We can't sit around here all day."

"What exactly do you plan to do? We no longer have a car, remember?"

"Don't need one."

"But—"

"If I had my way, you would stay right here until I could send someone for you. I doubt you'd let me get away with it. So you're either in or out, and I'm leaving. You have to decide if you're coming with me. Either way, I'll walk away with a clean conscience knowing I gave you the choice. Choose wrong and that's on your head, not mine."

This was the Dylan she remembered, rough around the edges but real. He wasn't the type to go behind a person's back and exact revenge. If Dylan saw someone mistreating a puppy, a senior citizen or a kid, he'd walk straight up to them and tell them what he planned to do right before he punched them in the teeth. He'd even let them know which fist was coming. No cleaning the toilet with an offender's toothbrush while he was out of the house. Dylan would wash out the guy's mouth with soap. No apologies.

"Okay. I'm coming with you. At least tell me where we're going."

"I'm going to find the bastard who kidnapped my daughter." Dylan shouldered his duffel, turned and walked out the door.

Chapter Five

"I know what I said before but we should go to the police now." Samantha followed Dylan out the door and onto the side street. He pulled a hat from his duffel and then tossed it back to her.

"No. I won't discuss your father with them." He shook his head as if for emphasis.

His phone had been buzzing the entire time. Word must be spreading. Dylan would deal with that when he got home.

He called the sheriff and gave a statement.

"Call him back," she pleaded. "I can tell them everything I know and that might help them find her."

"Absolutely not." He kept charging forward, setting a pace she could barely keep up with.

She jogged up to him and touched his shoulder. "I think—"

He spun around on her so fast she froze.

"As long as we find them first, I have a chance to get my daughter back unharmed. We make one wrong move and she's dead. The police have done nothing but make mistakes when it comes to anything connected to the Mason Ridge Abductor. I can't risk it with Maribel."

If anything happened to Dylan's little girl...

Samantha couldn't allow herself to think about it. She had to be positive.

"Contact whoever took her. Tell them we'll trade me for your daughter. I'm the one they want. She's innocent and shouldn't be involved in any of this."

"We do that and you're dead. I won't exchange one life for another no matter how desperate this situation seems. Besides, we don't know who's behind this or where they're keeping my daughter," he said.

"There's one way we might be able to find out. You said you have a friend who can hack into any device?"

Dylan nodded. His lips were so thin they almost disappeared.

"Then, have him do whatever he needs to in order to get into my father's phone. He isn't calling me back and that's not good. There might be a clue in his log."

"I already thought of that." He dismissed her suggestion with a wave of his hand as he turned. "It won't work. My contact already tapped into your line. The caller went to great lengths to hide his identity. He's not stupid."

There had to be some way to figure out who was behind this.

Dylan stopped. He surveyed the area, eyeing a motorcycle near the kitchen entrance to a restaurant. The metal-and-mesh screen door no doubt had been left open to let out heat from the ovens.

He motioned for Samantha to stay put, slipped inside and then returned a few minutes later with a helmet in hand. She had no idea how a man of his size could go unnoticed and was pretty certain the ability had been honed in his darker days. The idea of stealing didn't sit well with her, either.

"Get on."

She slid the helmet over her head and buckled the strap. It was a little too big for her but she didn't figure this was the time to argue with Dylan about who should be the one to wear it. Besides, even she knew that her state didn't require a helmet. Texas figured if a man was dumb enough to ride a motorcycle without one, they'd like to thin the herd.

"Take a stolen motorcycle out on the road and we'll be in jail before dinner," she said, tightening the strap.

"I bought it."

"Someone sold you their motorcycle just like that?"

"I can be very convincing when I need to be."

She had no doubt.

Dylan slid onto the seat in front of her. She leaned into him and wrapped her arms around his chest, remembering how frightened she'd been when he'd been shot earlier. Fear that had been all too familiar since this whole ordeal had begun. This past week had been the longest in her life, and the last thing she wanted to do was bring someone else into her problems. And yet having Dylan there brought a sense of calm to all this insanity.

The engine roared to life.

Dylan put his head down, shades on, and then weaved into the always heavy downtown Austin traffic.

Her body finally felt the weight of everything she'd been through in the past week. She didn't want to remember the last time she'd really slept, or had a decent meal, for that matter. She'd been surviving on power bars and water. The protein was enough to keep her going, and staying hydrated just seemed to make sense, but it was all robotic.

Lack of rest settled over her like a steel blanket, pressing down over already exhausted limbs.

By the time Dylan pulled into town, it was dark. Samantha figured no one would expect them to roll in on a motorcycle. The ride had been long but, thankfully, without incident. Kramer, or whoever was behind this, would have expected them to take I-35, but Dylan had taken 190 to I-45 and come up as though from Houston instead of Austin. His plan had proved brilliant even though it had added time they both knew they didn't have.

She recognized the storage facility on the edge of town where he stashed the Honda 500 as being fairly close to his small ranch.

"We can walk it from here," Dylan said, which were the first words that had passed between them in more than five hours. If he blamed her for Maribel's kidnapping, he didn't let on. His green eyes were sharper now, determined.

Her body ached from lack of sleep and little food. Even though her stomach growled, she couldn't imagine being able to hold down food. Not with what was at stake. Knowing a little girl's life—Dylan's little girl, at that—hung in the balance pretty much ensured Samantha couldn't have eaten or slept if she'd tried.

With the dark circles cradling Dylan's eyes, that was most likely all he could think about, too. Talking about how desperate the situation felt wouldn't change anything, wouldn't help matters. In fact, he needed a distraction.

"How far is your place?"

"About thirty minutes or so from here," he said.

He knew this area like the back of his hand, so she would rely on his skills to get them there safely.

The half-hour hike wasn't bad even through burning thighs. Dylan's silence was far more unnerving. Having grown up with three brothers, she knew that a quiet man was not a good sign.

It was black as pitch outside with no sign of light.

She listened for the sound of Dylan's footsteps and stopped a little too late, running into his back.

His hand found hers for the rest of the walk.

She couldn't have seen a tree if it was right in front of her face. His phone light appeared every once in a while, guiding them through the night.

They pushed through trees and brush, eventually making their way to the edge of a clearing. This had to be his place. An outside light was on over his carport and there were two others lighting the front of the small ranch-style house.

"We'll slip in through the back," he said. "Keep the lights off so we don't give anything away."

Samantha kept close even though he'd released her hand. She missed his warmth as soon as they disconnected.

They crept in through the back door.

The outdoor light permeated the large windows in the living room. With open blinds, she could see well enough not to walk into furniture. A few children's books along with several toys were on the sofa. Most everything else had a place and the room was in order, reminding her that Dylan was ex-military.

The place was full of simple, comfortable-looking furniture. A few framed snapshots of Dylan and Maribel had been placed on the fireplace mantel. Others were on side tables.

"Make yourself at home," he said, his voice a low rumble. "Shower's down the hall. There's a night-light always on in there and that should provide enough light for you to see. Fresh linens are in the closet. You need something to wear?"

She didn't want to ask why he would have women's clothes available, but the idea of a shower was too good to pass up. "I could stand to clean up. Fresh clothes would be nice."

"Go ahead. I'll put something on the counter." He paused a beat. "I'm sorry about earlier. I got heated and I shouldn't have—"

"You don't have to apologize. Under the circumstances, I thought you were pretty restrained, actually." She knew Dylan well enough to realize he wouldn't hurt her no matter how angry he was. Just like in high school, he needed space to think. The long drive home had most likely been what he'd needed to get his bearings again after the devastating news about Maribel.

"There's where you're wrong. I do have to say I'm sorry. I'm trying to be a better man since becoming a father."

"I hear what you're saying, Dylan. But I know you. You always were a good person even when you got in trouble before. I never doubted you for a second." She walked straight up to him, pressed up on her tiptoes and kissed his cheek.

He stood there for a second looking dumbfounded.

"Don't look so surprised. It's not as if I haven't known you since we were eleven years old." With that, Samantha walked out of the room, down the hall and into the bathroom.

She slipped out of her road-weary clothes and into the warm water.

Looking around at the couple of rubber toys and the princess bubble-bath bottle, Samantha figured this had to be Maribel's bathroom. Icy tendrils closed and squeezed around Samantha's heart, and her knees buckled. She caught herself with a hand on the wall and then said a silent prayer that Maribel would return home safely, just as Shane had. Any other outcome was unthinkable.

The shower rejuvenated her stiff muscles. She toweled off and picked up the clothes on the sink, a pair of boxers and a T-shirt. Definitely not women's wear. Why did that fact spread a glimmer of light into her heavy heart?

She put on the clothes, cinching the waist of the boxer shorts with a butterfly hair clip she found in the drawer.

No matter what else happened, Samantha was determined to help get Maribel back.

By the time she emerged from the bathroom, smells from the other room said there was food working in the kitchen. Her stomach growled in spite of the fact she couldn't imagine eating under the circumstances. It was impossible to think about doing anything normal while Dylan's daughter was missing.

Samantha made her way into the kitchen.

Dylan turned as she stepped into the room, stopped and stared. Moonlight streamed in from the window, casting dark shadows across his face.

"What?" She glanced down at her outfit self-consciously.

"Feel better?" His voice was low, gravelly.

"Much. Why? Do I look okay?"

He nodded.

"Sit down." He pointed toward the eat-in dining table and chairs.

"I'm not hungry."

"Eat anyway."

Giving short answers was another bad sign. Maybe

she could get him to open up and talk a little bit. It had always helped when her brothers were angry.

One look at Dylan, at his almost savage expression, told her he'd tear apart an animal with his bare hands if it meant getting his daughter back.

"What is she like? Maribel?"

"A ball of energy. More like a three-feet-tall tornado." A brief smile crossed his lips before he seemed to catch himself. "I don't want to talk about it right now."

Okay. She'd have to try a different tack. "Have you given any thought to our next move?"

"Yes."

"And?"

He pointed to the chair. "Sit."

"Okay." She did. So much for getting him to open up.

He walked over and set down a bowl of food and a fork in front of her.

"You know how to cook pasta?"

"It's Maribel's favorite. I learned." He picked up Samantha's arm and held it out. "You're losing weight."

That much was true, so she didn't argue.

"And you could barely hang on to me during the ride. I was afraid you'd fall off half the time."

She was almost surprised he'd noticed. Her grip around his broad chest had broken a time or two, but she'd quickly recovered. "Yes."

"So make the food in that bowl disappear," came out on a grunt.

She doubted the old Dylan would've noticed any of those things. He'd been all bad boy and, in a word, self-absorbed. But then, he'd had a lot of reasons to be. Life hadn't been easy or kind. The new Dylan, the one with a softer side, tugged at her heart even more. He'd always been handsome in that rugged, edgy, not-sure-what-to-expect way. And he'd always been unbreakable. Seeing this side to him—his Achilles' heel being his little angel—speared Samantha through the chest.

Since the reformed Dylan seemed determined to stand over her until she got a few bites down, she did so for the sake of show. The food tasted as good as it smelled, so she managed a few more. And she didn't want to like the small smile he conceded at the corners of his mouth that didn't reach his eyes—eyes that were tormented and angry.

That he seemed genuinely concerned about her well-being made her unable to disappoint him. He'd been a good friend so far. He'd put himself on the line to help her and she'd treated him like the enemy early on.

"Since we're throwing out apologies and all, I'm not sure if I thanked you earlier," she said, then forced down another bite.

"That's not an apology."

"Thank you anyway," she quipped.

He turned and walked to the counter near the sink, leaned his slender hip against the cabinet and scooped pasta into a second bowl. He stabbed the fork inside and then chewed the first bite. "If you're going to be strong enough to fight back, you need to eat."

She blinked up at him. Right again. And even though she absolutely knew that he had to be dying inside, he was just this tower of strength on the outside. His eyes gave away his pain, and she figured he was allowing her to see it. If he wanted to, he could go blank so as not to give away his advantage.

"For the record, I don't want to eat, either," he said, anger rolling off him in palpable waves, heating the room as he forced the fork into his dish again.

Dylan was right. She hadn't eaten a proper meal in the

past week or had a decent night of sleep. As it was, her left hand could scarcely hold the fork, let alone fight off an attacker. As much as she didn't want to eat or go to bed, a full belly would make her stronger and her head needed to hit that pillow soon.

He rinsed out his bowl and placed it in the dishwasher before returning to her side. She could feel him, even if she closed her eyes, standing next to her because Dylan was just this massive presence, a noticeable energy.

"What's the plan?" She couldn't suppress a yawn.

"Bed." He peered down at her bowl, removed the fork from her hand and swooped up the dish.

"There must be something else I can do to help."

He'd already turned his back to her. He didn't turn around. "Sleep."

"What will you do?"

"The same. I'll be no good to my daughter without grabbing a few hours of shut-eye. You need more than that." He started moving toward the sink again.

She wanted to protest, to argue that she was just as strong as he was, but it would have been pointless. And although she had every intention of pulling her own weight, she couldn't debate her need for sleep.

How on earth she'd get it, she had no idea. Being alone with Dylan was already doing all kinds of crazy things to her pulse. Adrenaline from the day had long dissipated and she was left with a beating heart in an exhausted body.

"Go brush your teeth. There's an extra toothbrush in the cabinet."

Under normal circumstances, she'd have been offended by the fact he'd resorted to using as few words as possible with her again. Except he was too much like her older brother Brent in that way. Brent would become laser focused and the little pleasantries went out the window. He'd said he didn't have time to fill his brain with nonsense when there was a serious task at hand. How many times had Brent come to the rescue in those early years after losing their mother? Too many.

She understood that, on some level, this was Dylan's way of coping.

And she couldn't find fault in that.

Before she could develop an argument for staying up, Dylan was at her side, urging her to stand.

"Lean on me," he said gruffly.

She didn't realize she needed him until she tried to stand on her own. Her knees buckled and his strong arm around her waist kept her from falling flat on her back.

Tired didn't begin to describe how she felt.

Brushing her teeth was the last thing she remembered doing.

THE HOUSE WAS still as Samantha's eyes flew open. She blinked a few times to gain her bearings. She was on the pullout sofa in a spare bedroom. He'd insisted she take his bed, but it hadn't seemed right to take that away from him. He needed sleep as much as she did, and he had a much better chance of getting it under the sheets he was used to. Besides, she barely even remembered closing her eyes before she was out.

What time was it?

She glanced around for a clock, got up and found one on a side table. Two o'clock in the morning. She'd gotten at least four hours of rest. That was more sleep than she'd had in the past week in its entirety. She'd take whatever she could get at this point. It was the little wins that mattered most right now. Celebrate all the little wins, her big brother would've told her, and that will keep you going even through the toughest of times.

It also sounded like something Dylan would say. And that was pretty much where his similarities with her older brother ended. The two were nothing alike physically. Brent was barely five feet ten inches. He had their father's small frame and their mother's brains. Thinking back, she remembered that her mother had been very bright. She'd also been artistic and had always checked the light in a room to decide where she would paint. She'd never asked for much. She'd carve out a niche in the brightest room she could find and keep a small cabinet with her art supplies there. While her mother might not have taken up much room in life, she'd occupied so much of Samantha's heart. Losing her had been a crushing blow.

She stuffed the thought down deep as she eased down the hallway toward Dylan's room. She'd have to pass his daughter's room to get there, and a coil tightened in her belly with each forward step.

The door decorated with the name Maribel was open, waiting.

As Samantha passed by, something dark and big caught her attention. Her eyes were still adjusting to the darkness, but she could see clearly enough to realize it was Dylan.

There he was, this big hulk of a man who had fallen asleep sitting on the floor of his daughter's room, leaning against the wall, holding on to a stuffed rabbit that was no doubt his daughter's favorite.

His head was slouched forward; he almost looked as if he was crying or praying. If she left him there like that, his neck would hurt in the morning. The least she could do was help him into a more comfortable position.

Samantha tiptoed inside and tried to ease the furry animal out of his hands.

In the next second, she was splayed out on her back and he was spread over top of her with a sharp object to her throat, his weight pressing her into the bamboo floor.

She'd scarcely seen the glimmer of metal before it was against her bare skin.

"Stop. It's me." She stared into dead eyes, a permanent sneer fixed on his face. Then it occurred to her. He was still asleep. One wrong move and he'd slit her throat before he woke. She kept her body very still. "Dylan. It's Samantha. Wake up. Please."

He snapped his head from side to side and then focused on her. "Dammit. That's a good way to get yourself killed."

He shifted his weight onto his right side and his groin pressed against her naked thigh. A volt of electricity trilled through her. She didn't want to feel that certain pull between them that made her remember that he smelled spicy and warm and windswept, and yet she couldn't deny its presence.

The anger and adrenaline coursed through her, igniting the sexual chemistry between them into passion and fire. He dipped his head and stopped when his lips barely touched hers.

Was he waiting for a sign that she wanted this to happen, too?

The knife hit the floor and she could hear it being pushed away, sliding across the bamboo.

"Samantha?" When he spoke, his lips brushed against hers and she could feel his breath, still minty from toothpaste.

"Yes" was all she could manage with him this close, with his body flush with hers and the material of his cargo pants against her thighs. That strong chest she'd been holding on to earlier moved up and down faster now, matching the rapid pace of her pulse.

"I've been thinking a lot about that kiss yesterday."

A dozen thoughts rushed her mind. She'd been thinking about it, too. More than she knew was good for her. She didn't want to like Dylan as more than a friend. Not now. Maybe never. This was all too complicated.

His soft lips pressed down on hers. Her hands came up and circled around his neck. He tasted so good.

He was propped up on one elbow and his free hand started roaming as he deepened the kiss. He was touching, feeling, connecting, and all she could think was *more*.

And then it dawned on her.

He was searching for comfort. It could have been any woman underneath him right then. The two of them were friends. Period.

She broke the kiss and slid out from underneath him. He didn't immediately move, as though he needed a few seconds to process her actions.

"I was out of line there."

"No. I wanted it to happen, too. But that's not good for either one of us." She started to say *right now* but stopped herself. The truth was there might never be a right time for the two of them, and she had no intention of confusing a friendship for something else again.

"You're right." Those two words stung. Had she been hoping he'd argue?

"Won't happen again." He pushed up onto his knees, then stood. "You want a glass of water?"

She shook her head, embarrassed. She'd let things between them go too far, and now it would be awkward. Dylan wasn't reaching out to her because he liked her;

it was because of the tension he was under. He needed a release. Sex with Dylan would blow her mind, she was sure. But then what?

It would get weird between them, just as it had in college when she'd been a shoulder to cry on for the crush she picked up during Freshman Lit. Jude Evers had been busy working his way through college, a single dad with two young kids. He'd caught his fiancée in bed with his best friend. He and Samantha had bonded over the really crappy espressos at the student union that were like mud in a cup. The two had become friends, then lovers, and she'd put her heart on the line with him. Hadn't that turned out to be a mistake? She'd babysat his kids so he could go to the student union to study, or so she'd thought. Boredom had gotten the best of her after she'd put his kids to bed, so she'd logged on to social media.

There he was, caught on camera kissing another girl from class, no less. He was shirtless, and the reason why was pretty obvious. They'd just made love.

Samantha had never felt so used.

When she'd confronted him that night, he'd said he thought they had an understanding—that the two of them were friends with benefits.

Embarrassment had threatened to consume her. If it hadn't been too late to drop the class, she would have been first in line. Instead, she'd had to sit through ten weeks of analyzing prose with him and the other woman.

The worst part had been saying goodbye to the kids she'd grown to love.

Samantha pushed up off the floor. At least she could try to get a few more hours of sleep. Although with Dylan's bedroom two doors down, she doubted she'd be able to completely relax.

He appeared in the doorway as she took a step toward

it, and she gasped. That man could be stealthy when he needed to be.

"Sorry about a few minutes ago," he said, and his voice was still gravelly. "I got carried away in the moment, but I'm good now. It was a boundary that shouldn't have been crossed."

This was *supposed* to be exactly what she wanted to hear…so what was up with the stinging feeling in her chest?

Chapter Six

Dylan had been resting his eyes in his daughter's room for a good half hour before Samantha had caught him off guard. Kissing her the first time had been a mistake. The second had been sloppy. Sure, he felt an attraction sizzle every time she walked into a room. The only thing that proved was that he was still a man aware of a beautiful woman.

He'd had just enough of a power nap to fuel him for the day ahead and get his head on straight. Being a full-time father to Maribel was the greatest job he'd ever had and he wouldn't trade a minute of it. Caring for his little angel 24/7 left little time for anything else in his life. There were no regrets. Being her father was the best thing that had ever happened to him. But there was no time for detours, or *anyone* else in his life.

Besides, Samantha was a friend. Sure, she gave him signals. And they had chemistry. Again, it was down to man and woman, primal urges and all that. He'd been seeking proof of life and so had she. They'd been through hell together, so hormones had gotten out of control.

They most likely wouldn't go away anytime soon, either. So he'd have to work a little harder to keep them under wraps.

Besides, Dylan Jacobs didn't "do" relationships. He

also didn't engage in flings, not since he'd screwed his head on straight a few years back, and especially not since Maribel had shown up.

His feelings for Samantha were nothing more than a snag he could deal with. The last thing he needed right now was another complication in his life. His hands were full with the serious situation he found himself in. And it would take all his energy to remain focused on the jerk who'd taken his baby girl. Once he got her back, his days would be filled with work and play and preschool.

Besides, there were about three females he trusted, and one of them was three feet tall. The other two had been carefully screened during the interviewing process: his housekeeper and the preschool headmaster.

Dylan shook off his emotions as he moved to the bathroom for a cold shower.

Fifteen minutes later, he walked into the kitchen. As soon as it was daylight, he needed to swing by the sheriff's office and see what kind of leads they were following through on. More than anything else, he needed to come up with his own plan to find Maribel.

At the moment, all he had to go on was the name Thomas Kramer. A dead man couldn't kidnap a child. Whoever it was had to have enough money and connections to fund the recent attacks. That led Dylan to believe there could be some sort of crime ring involved. Seemed as though there was a story in the national news at least once a week about child abduction rings, and it would take serious money to pull off having a crew in Austin and in Mason Ridge to pursue them. Kramer might've been involved in a bigger organization.

On a related topic, there was the matter of finding Samantha's father. Involving her more than Dylan needed to was a bad idea for more reasons than just his growing feelings toward her. His best chance to find her father rested on her, though, so there was no choice but to keep her close and in the loop. For now.

If the man behind all this had gotten to her father, he wouldn't have taken Maribel. His daughter wouldn't be harmed as long as Mr. Turner was on the run.

Other than that, he had precious little to go on and no way to find his baby. Dylan refused to think about how scared she must be right now. Or that this was the first night she'd spent away from home since she'd come to live with him a year ago. His hands fisted as he checked the clock. Nearly two hours had passed since the incident with Samantha. Time was not his friend.

He ignored how empty the house felt without Maribel in it. Instead of focusing on the negative, he booted up his laptop, located a pen and paper in the kitchen and then wrote the name Thomas Kramer in the center.

The next name he wrote was Samantha's father's, Henry Turner. He circled both names and drew a line connecting them. What did her father know? He put Samantha's name on top and then his own across from hers. From his, he drew a dotted line downward and then scribbled his daughter's name.

The sheriff's office didn't know about the link to Mr. Turner, at least not yet.

So far, they thought they were looking for a lost girl, not a kidnapping case. No matter how desperate he was to get his daughter back, he couldn't risk involving the law yet.

There had to be another way, a connection he was missing.

Talking to Samantha's father was a top priority. Finding him would be the challenging part. His house would most likely be a dead end. He'd know better than to stay there. Where else did he like to go?

How about the hardware store that he owned? Mr. Turner wouldn't likely be there, because it was too obvious, but Dylan wanted to know what the hours were so he could drop by and ask a few questions to Mr. Turner's employees. Dylan located his cell and called the number.

The recording said the place didn't open for another five hours.

Dylan ended the call and then jotted down the time. Surely Mr. Turner wouldn't be stupid enough to walk in the front door of his shop. He'd have to get someone to open for him, though, or people would get suspicious.

Where else had Samantha said her father liked to go?

He was a fisherman, so he would know all the area lakes. There were dozens of good spots in North Texas alone, depending on what he liked to fish. She'd already mentioned catfish. Dylan wrote down the words *fishing cabin* with a question mark. Mr. Turner might have a few secret hiding spots that only his daughter would know about. Dylan would ask Samantha as soon as she stirred.

In the meantime, he could send a few emails to his buddies with an update. His inbox was already loaded with concerned friends reaching out to him. Samantha had given out his number to her father, whom the kidnappers might already have found. Again, Dylan guessed they hadn't.

There were twenty messages in his spam folder. Every once in a while there was something useful in there, so he opened the folder. He scanned the usual scam emails.

Midway down the list, his eye stopped on one. It was an invitation of some sort.

Knowing he might regret his actions when a new virus blacked out his screen or some other irreversible nonsense occurred to his laptop, he took a chance and opened it anyway. It had arrived in his inbox within an hour of Maribel's kidnapping.

The heading read Want to Trade?

Red-hot fury licked through his veins, burning his skin from the inside out.

Dylan clicked on the message.

There was a meet-up spot. 1212 Whistle Bend Road, Mason Ridge, Texas. And a request to bring the *Brave* Barbie doll from the second shelf in his daughter's room. He pushed off the counter and made a beeline to Maribel's room.

Had that bastard been inside Dylan's house? In his daughter's room?

Anger roared through him as he stalked to her bookshelf. She never played with her *Brave* doll. Maribel kept it on her bookshelf as a reminder to be strong.

Had they taken more of Maribel's things? Dylan hadn't thought of that before. He began checking her drawers. Whoever had been in the house had been careful not to leave a trace. There wouldn't likely be fingerprints, either. This guy was good at covering his tracks. Should this situation go south, he'd make sure the son of a bitch paid dearly.

Her favorite pajamas were missing, along with a couple outfits. Someone had gone to great lengths to make sure she had supplies.

When he really looked around, he saw that a few other things were gone, too. Several of her toys had disappeared. Dylan scooped her favorite bunny, Rofurt, off the floor.

He held the stuffed animal as he moved to the laptop. Someone who went to the pains to take the child's personal items couldn't intend to harm her. Could they?

His first real sense of hope bloomed. He was cautious not to be too optimistic, understanding he wanted her back so badly that his mind would look for any positive sign to latch on to, real or imagined. He didn't want to kid himself.

He immediately pulled up the address on Google Maps and switched to Earth mode. There was a semiwooded lot with nothing on the front of the property but a mailbox. Anyone could stay hidden in the nearby tree line, watching.

Dylan's next call was to Jorge. He was the only person Dylan figured he wouldn't be disturbing in the middle of the night.

Jorge picked up on the second ring. "What can I do for you, my man?"

"I need you to track down an IP address. I got an email."

"On it." The sound of Jorge's fingers tapping on the keyboard came through the line. He already had been given access to Dylan's accounts when they'd first started working together.

"Also, I need information on the location."

"Name it." The staccato sound stopped.

"I want to know who owns that piece of property. Can you expedite that for me?"

"You know I'd do anything. Does this have to do with...?"

Dylan was relieved Jorge didn't finish the question. Jorge would've seen the Amber Alert and known Maribel was missing. He didn't need to hear those words from anyone. "Yeah."

"I'm on it right now. Call you back in a minute?"

"I'll keep the phone in my hand."

The call ended and Dylan stared at the piece of paper

with the names. What was he missing? What possible connection could any of these people have to each other?

SAMANTHA TOSSED AND TURNED. Again. Sleep was about as close as New York to Texas, and neither had a fast track to the other. She peeled off the sheet and tiptoed to her door.

If Dylan was awake, he was quiet.

She pushed thoughts of his body pressed to hers out of her head as she opened the door and walked into the hallway. She heard typing noises coming from the kitchen area. He had to be up.

The promise of freshly brewed coffee kept her feet moving toward the scent. She didn't want to surprise him, so she relaxed into a normal pace and cleared her throat.

Turning the corner, she immediately noticed his tense posture. He was leaned over his laptop, intensely studying the screen. She wasn't sure he'd heard her walk into the room.

"That coffee I smell?" she asked softly. The only light came from the glow of his screen.

His gaze didn't waver. "Help yourself."

What could have possibly happened in the middle of the night?

Samantha easily located a mug and then poured a cup. She took a sip, enjoying the burn on her throat, the taste of the dark roast.

Tension sat thickly in the air, and she hoped it wasn't because of what had happened between them earlier. She wouldn't get through any of this without Dylan.

"Can I pour you another cup while I'm in here?" she asked as a peace offering.

He grunted something that sounded like an affirmation.

As she returned with a full mug, his head snapped up

and his gaze focused on her. He spun the laptop around so that she could read the screen.

Fear exploded through her as she read the email.

Next, Dylan produced a list of everyone they knew. She recognized all the names of their friends and the half dozen or so older boys.

"You think one of our friends could be involved?"

He steepled his fingers. "It's possible, or they might have seen something that could help us figure out who else is."

"At least we have a direction now," she said. She nodded toward the laptop, knowing he was grasping at straws. "When do they want to make the exchange?"

"Midnight tomorrow."

"I wonder why they're giving us so much time."

"My guess is that they're hoping to find your father first. Maybe they think they're close."

"This doesn't give us enough time to prepare." She took another sip of fresh coffee.

Samantha planned to personally see to it that Maribel returned home safe. The question was whether or not she should split up from Dylan to make it happen. The thought of doing any of this without him made her shoulders tense.

"Hungry?" She moved to the kitchen, needing something to do with her hands or she'd go crazy.

He made a move to get up. She held her hand up to stop him.

"No. I got this." She opened the fridge. "Let's see what we have to work with in here."

DYLAN WANTED TO talk to Samantha about more than just food. He wanted to tell her that everything would work out and that they'd be fine. The words fell dead on his tongue. Putting much thought into doing anything besides getting Maribel back was near impossible.

They also needed to find her dad before the other guys did. The sun would be up in an hour or so. He figured they could leave before first light.

If Dylan was a betting man, he'd put his money on the fact that the property would be near one of the sheds where Rebecca and her brother had been held when they'd been kidnapped fifteen years ago. Everyone knew Brody had torn one of them down. Hell, Dylan had been right there alongside his buddy, shredding the cursed building.

"Where should we start looking for my father?" Samantha pulled out what looked like the fixin's to make a country-style omelet.

"At the beginning," he said, trying to analyze how they'd get through the woods and to the shed area unseen to scope out the place.

"What are we missing? We know Kramer's name is being thrown out there to distract us. Right?" she asked.

"Whoever's doing this is twisted. Maybe Kramer wasn't even the bloody fool who'd taken Rebecca and Shane in the first place. We might have it all wrong."

"Whoever is behind this must have some money or connections."

"I thought about that, too. The men in Austin were most likely hired guns."

"Where's a knife?" She laid out an onion and bell peppers on the counter.

"The top drawer to your left. There's a safety lock on it," he said.

She fumbled with trying to open it.

He moved beside her. She smelled like Maribel's favorite flowers, lilies. It was the shampoo he kept in her bathroom, which was also shared with guests. Maribel had picked it out for when Ms. Anderson stayed overnight. He'd also seen it as a sign his daughter wished there were a woman in the house on a more permanent basis.

As much as he wanted to be Maribel's world, he acknowledged that he was limited on what he could teach her due to a severe lack of estrogen. He filled in the gaps with Ms. Anderson and Mrs. Applebee, knowing full well there would come a day when Maribel needed more than he could provide.

He'd cross that bridge when he came to it. In order to have a relationship with a woman, he'd have to trust her. And thanks to his mother's disappearing act, that wasn't likely. He always disconnected with a relationship when it came down to it. Even though Lyndsey had had her reasons for lying, Dylan had loved her. He'd been devastated when she'd suddenly accepted a new job and moved to New Mexico without leaving an address. She'd gone to great lengths to keep him out of her life.

His stubborn streak had kicked in, saying he didn't go where he wasn't wanted. He'd taken the hint and walked away.

How many times had he regretted that action since then? How many times had he wished he could go back and get those precious few years with Lyndsey back? He would've tracked her down and sat on her stoop until she'd been forced to listen to his side.

A big part of him wished Lyndsey was still around, and not just for Maribel's sake. He and Lyndsey had enjoyed each other's company and had great sex, and everything else could have been built from there. Lots of relationships had weaker foundations than fantastic sex, easy conversation and a great kid.

Then again, if Lyndsey had still been alive, he might

not even have known he had a daughter. This was the kind of mixed blessing that defined his life.

And he couldn't ignore reality. What kind of relationship could they have had if they didn't talk about anything important? Conversation must not have been her forte, because she hadn't even had one with him to let him know he was a father.

Dylan wished she'd known him well enough, trusted him enough to attempt to coparent together. Had he really been such a jerk that she'd never considered letting him in on her secret? She'd known about his background. While he hadn't wanted kids, she had to have known he wouldn't have turned his back on his child, either. If Lyndsey had known anything about him, she should've known that.

He shook off his reverie as he stood next to Samantha.

Trips down memory lane didn't change a thing. He should know. After losing Lyndsey, he'd taken a bunch of them.

"Here. You open the drawer just a little, then press this plastic piece down." His arm grazed Samantha's, causing electric impulses to fire through him. He didn't want to think about how soft her skin was, or those slender, long legs being right next to him. How much she trembled when he stood close.

Or how well she'd fit him earlier when she was underneath him.

He was pretty sure any of those things would wreck a friendship faster than a mosquito bite itched.

Samantha hesitated for just a second before gripping the wooden knife handle.

Dylan took a step back, then took his seat at the breakfast bar as she went to work chopping the green bell peppers. She seemed to know her way around the kitchen, and he caught himself staring at her fluid movements.

What the hell?

He chalked up his being sentimental to watching too many Disney movies with Maribel. They were making him soft.

Dylan Jacobs needed another person in his life like dry grass needed a lit match.

Chapter Seven

The second Dylan's ringtone sounded, Samantha's heart raced. It was bad enough that every time he was near, her pulse quickened. And that every time he touched her, awareness skittered across her skin.

And now every sound had her on edge.

She'd been jumping at shadows for a solid week. Every time she thought she saw something move, her stomach lurched. She exhaled slowly and refocused on the pan in front of her, turning the omelet.

"Yes, sir. She's right here," Dylan said. His voice carried a sense of foreboding. She turned off the heat on the stove and set the pan aside.

"It's for you." Her heart dropped to her toes when he turned and caught her gaze. One look in his eyes said there was trouble. "It's your father."

She studied Dylan's expression carefully as they met in the middle of the kitchen.

"Daddy?" she said into the receiver.

"Don't say anything to anyone. You hear? Don't let them get to you. I'm going to fix this," her father said. Rustling noises came through the line.

"To who? Fix what? What are you talking about?" She listened closely, trying to identify a noise that might give away his location.

A crack sounded, followed by a grunt, and she couldn't breathe.

Fear roared through her, causing her hands to shake.

"That's not what you're supposed to say to her. I thought we had an understanding," a male voice said.

"Daddy? What's going on? Where are you?" Questions fired out frantically. Her heart pounded in her chest as she looked straight at Dylan.

"Try to keep him on the line for as long as you can," Dylan whispered. He'd already picked up his landline and was making a call. Dylan was the picture of focus.

She figured he was calling his technical contact to see if they could get a trace.

"Hello? Who's there? Talk to me, Daddy. I can't help you if you won't tell me what's going on," she said quietly. The silence on the other end was deafening. "Tell me who is doing this to you."

"I tried to run but they found me" came through on a raspy, winded breath. "I know what's really going on and it's big, he's big. It's—" More shuffling noises came through the phone and her father screamed.

Her entire body began to shake.

"Please don't hurt him. Who is it, Daddy? Who's hurting you?" Desperation sat like an anchor in her stomach.

This was so not good. Her father was getting older, and no way would he be able to protect himself against younger, stronger men.

"Daddy. Are you there?" She said a quick prayer that her father would be all right. She couldn't imagine life if anything happened to him. The two of them had been the closest. And he hadn't been perfect but she'd always known that he'd been the best father he could be, especially when he'd had to step in to be a mother, too. And even though it was Samantha's fault her mother was dead, her dad had never once made her feel that way. He wasn't that kind of person. How on earth could he have gotten himself into this kind of serious trouble?

"They already know I confessed everything to you," he said loudly, through labored breathing. Then he whispered, "They won't hurt me as long as they can't find you."

A thousand fears raced through her all at once, and at least a dozen scenarios of ways they might torture him.

"Daddy?" What could she do? Call Brent? If she could get ahold of her brothers, would they know what to do? She needed her father too much for anything to happen to him.

More sounds of struggle came over the line before it went dead.

"Oh, no. No!" A heavy weight pushed down on her as she looked toward Dylan. "This isn't real. This can't be happening. They're going to kill him."

Dylan ended his call. "I have someone all over this. Maybe we'll get lucky this time and get a location. We'll know something in a few minutes."

"And then what? Go to him? They found him. They're going to kill him. He'll be dead by the time we start the car." Panic was getting the best of her and she knew it. She needed to take a few deep breaths and calm down. Except that was her father out there. Alone. And he didn't deserve to die by the hands of some jerk, no matter what her father had seen or did fifteen years ago.

She relayed what her father had told her.

"Now we know for certain why they've been looking for you," Dylan said quickly.

"But I have no idea what my father knows," she said quickly.

"They don't know that. He said that for leverage."

She paced back and forth in the kitchen. "But they will kill him. He might be dead already."

"If they wanted to kill him right away, then why not shoot him and stuff him in the back of the car? Why subdue him? They're using him to get to you. Once they tie up that loose end, they have no need to keep anyone alive."

His words, as direct as they were, did their job well. He was right and she couldn't come up with an argument to his point.

Samantha thought about Dylan's words as she stalked back and forth in the kitchen. "He said this whole thing is bigger, that he's bigger."

"Meaning Thomas Kramer was only a small part of it, like we suspected."

"Daddy was clear." She stopped for a second. "This nightmare just won't end."

"There's only one thing we can do."

"And that is?"

"Scout out the meet-up location and then wait."

WHEN DYLAN'S PHONE RANG, he snatched it off the table, in part to stop himself from walking straight over to Samantha and pulling her into his arms. The last thing he needed was for this situation to get stickier than it already was, and he shouldn't get any closer to her than he felt. Being there for each other during a difficult time was one thing. Friends did that without question. There was something else going on between them and that was sending him into a tailspin. One he didn't have time or energy for.

"What do you have for me?" he asked Jorge after checking the screen.

"Good news. I figured out who owns the plot of land for the address you gave me. Sort of."

"What does that mean?"

"Whoever owns it is smart enough not to use a traceable company."

"Are you saying there's a dummy corporation in place?"

"The one listed is offshore," Jorge confirmed, "making it that much more difficult to pinpoint."

"Any chance you can figure out who owns it?"

"Can a retriever bring back a ball? Of course I can. It'll take time, though. These things are like peeling an onion once you dig into them. The best are smart enough to put up a lot of layers."

"What about the call that came in on my cell a few minutes ago? Did you pick up anything on that?"

"That's easy. That came from a pay phone at a gas station near Eagle Lake," Jorge supplied.

Dylan repeated the information to Samantha.

"Daddy likes to fish there sometimes. It's not his favorite spot, but he's been there once or twice." Her mind looked to be clicking through the possibilities.

"Which is smart. He'd know the area fairly well but most people wouldn't associate him with that place when they thought of him leaving town."

"True. You'd have to be really close to him in order to figure that out."

"Who might know about this other than you and your brothers?"

"My brothers wouldn't know. Only me. I'm the one who fishes with him. My brothers haven't gone since we were kids. It was sort of mine and Dad's thing. I think he did it to make me feel special after my mom…" Her tone changed when she spoke about her mother. He'd noticed it before. There was a subtle shift. He doubted she would tell him what it meant even if he asked outright.

He turned toward the cell in his hand. "What about the IP address? Get anything there?"

"Sorry, man. It's a dead end," Jorge said.

Dylan thanked his friend and ended the call.

"Eagle Lake is not that far—less than a half hour's drive from here." Dylan grabbed his keys from the counter. "We'll head out as soon as you're dressed."

It took Samantha only three minutes to throw on the clothes he'd had Rebecca drop off for her, pull her hair up in a ponytail and walk into the living room with an expression that said she was ready.

Even wearing running shorts and an athletic shirt, she was stunning.

"Think he'll still be anywhere near there?" she said as she followed him into the kitchen and toward the back door.

"I doubt it, but there's no way to know for sure unless we chance it. I want to ask around. See if anyone saw anything. Maybe we can get a description of the person or persons who took him." Dylan grabbed Rofurt. For reasons he didn't want to examine, he laced his and Samantha's fingers and led her out the door. His sport-utility was parked out back. He surveyed the area as they stepped outside.

The first light would break the horizon in an hour, which gave them just enough time to slip out of town in the dark.

"Think we should split up? Would that make things easier?" Samantha asked.

The question caught him off guard as he opened the door for her. He glanced at the empty car seat in the back and a coil tightened in his stomach. He clenched his teeth.

"We need to stick together. It's our best hope of finding either of them." Since Maribel's kidnapping was connected to Mr. Turner, Dylan planned to be glued to Samantha. Besides, she was the missing piece. They got her and it was game over.

He moved to the driver's side, took his seat and fired up the engine.

Neither spoke on the half-hour-long drive to the gas station where her father made the call.

"Do you have a picture of him in your purse?" Dylan parked near the pay phone.

"No. I ditched my phone a long time ago. That's the only place I have... Wait a minute. My phone automatically updates to storage in a cloud. I can give you the password and you can get in."

"Good." Dylan handed his phone to her.

"We were fishing two weeks ago and I snapped something... There." She held up the screen. Her father had a decent-size fish on the line.

"Show that around inside."

"Think they'll ask questions about his disappearance? I don't want to make it worse for him if someone gets the bright idea to call the police."

"Tell him he's been forgetful lately and that he might've wandered off. Say you're heading to the police station next."

Samantha agreed and then disappeared inside the store.

Dylan searched the grounds for anything that might help, any clue that might assist him in finding her father and, dare he hope, his Maribel. He didn't want to think about how scared she might be right then.

Anger tightened the coil.

He fisted his hands and focused on the ground as Samantha stalked toward him.

"Any luck?" he asked, instantly regretting his word choice. Luck was for slot machines.

"No one has seen him."

He'd feared as much. It would've been dark and this area was known for fishing. No one would've thought much about a man in a truck. "Hey. Wait a minute. If your dad was out here, where's his truck?"

"That's a good point. Wouldn't they have taken it?" she asked.

"If they did, there had to be at least two of them. Maybe they didn't want to cause a stir when the truck was left overnight." Dylan searched the ground for tracks, heel marks, anything that might indicate they were in the right spot.

Stepping lightly, he noticed a thick line in the gravel. "Come over here."

Samantha did. "What is it?"

"What does that look like to you?"

"It's the size of the heel of a boot." She gasped. "Daddy?"

"Could be. Looks like the person might have been dragged over here." He pointed to a boot imprint. "Might've gained his footing here."

The trail stopped.

Glancing a few feet away, he saw tire tracks. "This looks suspicious, doesn't it?"

"They went in this direction." Samantha's line of sight traveled away from the boot imprint.

"Took him in his own truck," Dylan said. "They must've had another vehicle here."

"He said he knows what really happened all those years ago, and all I keep thinking is how can that be if he wasn't involved? If he wasn't out there that night? It would make sense. He was drinking back then. Cleaned up his act after... Maybe he was so shaken up by what he'd done he started walking the straight and narrow?"

"Doesn't mean he was part of it." Dylan didn't say that his reassurance meant very little, and the look she gave him said she appreciated him for it.

"He wasn't home a lot during that time. He'd stay out after the shop closed and drink. I thought he was going to disappear like my mom, so I'd wait up for him. I could tell something was wrong with him but I didn't know what. I thought he was sick or something, so I asked Trevor."

Dylan was so caught off guard that she was opening up to him. "That's how you found out he'd been drinking? From your brother?"

"Trevor sat me down and explained to me how much Daddy loved our mother. That her dying had been difficult for him and that we should cut him some slack. I felt so betrayed and so stupid. How did Trevor know all this but I didn't?"

"He was older, for one."

"True, but he had his own life. I was closer to Daddy than the boys were. Or so I thought."

"Your father was trying to protect you."

"That's exactly what Trevor said. How did you know that?"

"I have a daughter. And it's the easiest way to get to me, which was most likely the reason they tried to take you in the first place. Everyone knows you and your father have always been close."

"I saw you with her at the grocery last week."

"Why didn't you say anything?"

"You looked as though you had your hands full."

He cracked a smile. "She keeps me busy, that's for

sure. But I don't bite and neither does she, no matter what her teacher says. False accusations."

"Did you teach her to do that to keep boys away?"

"Not yet. I figure I have a few years before I have to start worrying about them. And then I'm not too concerned. I have weapons." He chuckled, and it felt good to release some of the tension knotting inside him. "You could've said something in the store."

"What? It's not as if we've kept in touch since high school."

"We knew each other."

"I remember you getting into a lot of trouble. What happened to change that?"

"The US Army. They gave me a brotherhood. Taught me life was about more than myself and my problems."

"You ever hear from your folks?"

"No."

"Well, they're missing out. Maribel is a doll. I could seriously pinch those cheeks for days. And that curly hair. Who could miss out on such an adorable thing?"

"I did. For a while," he said.

"I wondered what had happened."

Dylan wasn't prepared to talk about Lyndsey to anyone. Not yet anyway. If he was going to talk about her, then Samantha would be exactly the kind of person he could see himself opening up to. He just wasn't the type, or maybe this wasn't the time. "It's long over. I didn't even know about Maribel until last year."

"I'd heard you bought your ranch a little more than a year ago. Dad's a bit of a gossip in his old age. He's lonely, I think. I wish he'd found someone to spend time with. He just withered away after Mom. Honestly, I was surprised to find out you had a daughter."

"You and me both," he said a little more curtly than

he'd planned. Talking about the past was opening old wounds—wounds he didn't want to think about right then.

She seemed to take the hint, and kept quiet as they walked the perimeter of the parking lot.

He saw something out of the corner of his eye. Might be nothing, so he didn't want to raise the alarm just yet and get Samantha's hopes up unnecessarily.

On closer look, there was a phone on the ground. He picked it up and examined it. There was a picture of a bass on the protective cover. "What kind of phone does your father have?"

"An iPhone. Why?"

"Any special markings on it?"

"Yeah. What do you have?" Her eyes grew wider as she moved closer. "He has that picture on his phone. That has to be his."

The battery had been pulled out. Dylan fished his own phone out of his pocket. Since it was the same model, the battery should work in both. He popped it in.

Several text messages had gone unanswered from the boys and Samantha. "Have you been helping out at the store lately?"

"Sometimes."

"Has anyone been in that you didn't recognize? Anyone talking to your father on the side?"

"No. Not that I can think of off the top of my head."

Dylan searched through pictures, stopping on the last few. "Your dad may have just told us who was after him."

"Those guys are wearing security uniforms. Wait. I recognize the outfits. Do they work for Charles Alcorn?" His name had a habit of showing up in connection with the crime, usually in a positive way. "That's the security uniform for his company. They might be posing as employees, trying to fly under the radar. People wouldn't bat an eyelash at someone who works for Alcorn. Does your father have any dealings with him? Get any supplies from one of his companies?"

"None that I know of. That's so weird. You know, I have seen that guy in the store." She pointed at the guy on the left, who had a big build, light hair and a beard. "He was there a couple Saturdays ago asking for my dad. I overheard from the stockroom. Dad said he was going fishing. Who knows what he was doing now?" A look flashed behind her eyes that Dylan told himself to ask about later. He couldn't pinpoint the emotion and he didn't think it had anything to do with her father's disappearance.

Dylan forwarded the pictures to his secure phone line in case someone was watching Mr. Turner's line. "We figure out who these guys are and we might get lucky with a connection."

Chapter Eight

Samantha rubbed her temples to stave off a splitting headache as Dylan pulled out of the parking lot. Her brain felt as if it might explode. "How do you intend to find out who those guys are?"

"Jorge can help figure it out. If they really do have security jobs, then they've been through some kind of screening process. That'll make his job a lot easier. He can hack into almost any system except law enforcement."

"Can't or won't?"

Good call. "Won't. And I'd never ask. I find that I get a lot more information playing nice than breaking the law. That I only do when I have no other choice. I don't think we're going to find anything else here."

"Where to next?" The way he'd talked about his daughter a few minutes ago had nearly cracked her heart in two pieces. There'd been a softness to his voice she'd never heard before, and his entire disposition had changed. And there'd been something that looked a lot like love in his expression.

Samantha knew firsthand how important a dad's love was to a girl. It would define every future relationship she had with a man.

"Can I ask you something?" Dylan secured his seat belt at the same time she did.

"Sure."

"You don't have to answer. It's really none of my business."

"Go ahead. What's the worst that can happen?" she asked, still massaging her temples.

He pulled the sport-utility onto the stretch of highway. "Your father lied to you when you were a kid. That had to make you angry."

"Yeah. Of course."

"But you forgave him?" he asked.

"Yes."

"Why?"

She shrugged. "Because deep down he's a good person."

"You think liars are good people?"

"Life's not black-and-white to me. No one's perfect. Surely you understand that after what you went through when you were younger. You made mistakes, but that doesn't make you a bad person." The sincerity in her words impressed him.

"The only good thing about me is Maribel."

"That's not true. She might bring out the best in you but the good was always there," she said matter-of-factly.

"I'm not so sure about that." Was it true, though? Mostly Dylan remembered being angry when he was younger. He'd been so furious with the world when he was a kid that he'd thought he might literally burst into flames from the inside out. The military had seemed a better place to take out his anger, and he'd known on some level that he needed the discipline. He'd been paddling in a sea of anger and self-hate before finding his true brotherhood in the military. As a kid, he'd blamed his parents' rejection on himself. He'd figured he had to be one pretty messed-up kid if his own parents didn't like him. Gram had reacted with an iron fist, and that had gone over like battery acid in a punch bowl. Dylan had rebelled even more, and then she'd died while he was in Afghanistan, before he'd had the chance to tell her he was sorry. If he could go back...

"You don't have to be. I saw it before in you and I see it now."

"And what is *it*, exactly?"

"I was in trouble and you refused to turn your back on me. Even when I tried to push you away. What does that say about you?"

"You kicked me in the groin," he said flatly.

"I'm still sorry about that, by the way." She smiled weakly.

"That's okay. But I still haven't forgiven you," he joked, trying to loosen the knot tightened in his gut.

"Great. Now I've gone and reminded you of the whole thing."

"We've had better moments since then." He was thinking about her soft skin. Dylan had a weakness for great legs, and hers were perfect, long, silky and sexy. He'd like to start at the ankles and kiss his way up to the insides of her thighs. There were other things about her that he found increasingly difficult to push out of his mind. The curve at the small of her back where his hand had rested earlier gave way to a taut waist that blended into soft hips. Dylan wouldn't mind spending a little time touching her, exploring her long curves, kissing her. He couldn't remember the last time a kiss had rocketed his pulse like the two they'd already shared. And that was just the icing on the cake. Appreciation of her real beauty came from looking into her eyes and seeing a whole different world he wanted to get lost in. Samantha was sharp, intelligent and *dangerous*, he reminded himself.

"Can I ask you something else?"

"Go ahead."

"How'd you take it when you lost your mom? You were older than Maribel. I honestly don't know how to explain any of this to her. I tell her that her mother is in heaven, whatever that is, and I'm not even sure if she realizes that means she'll never see her again. To her thinking, heaven might be some place, like Florida, where moms go on vacation and don't come home from."

"Be honest with her. You don't have to explain it to her like you're talking to me but she deserves to know the truth, that her mother isn't coming back."

"I know. Damn. For the first six months of the year all she said was 'Mama?' every time someone came to the door. She'd run, expectant, as if she'd been at the babysitter's all day and it was finally time to come home. There were tears, too. She cried herself to sleep for weeks calling out for her mother in the night." He stopped to gain control of his emotions.

"What did you do?"

"I'd settle in next to her and tell her that her mother was in heaven."

"Like I said, tell her the truth. Mom's not coming back, but that doesn't mean she doesn't still love you or want to be with you. Use whatever language is age appropriate but be honest. The worst feeling in the world would be thinking that a mother would come back once she was gone. Tell her that her mother would come back if she could. That she didn't want to leave her. And most of all, tell her that none of this is her fault." Samantha's hands started trembling. "It's not her fault," she repeated.

Dylan turned on his signal, changed lanes and then

pulled over to the side of the road to park. He turned off the engine. He reached across the seat for her. The pain in her eyes was a knife to his chest. "Losing your mother wasn't your fault, either. Accidents happen and take away people we love and there isn't a damn thing anyone can do about it except enjoy the time we have together, make it mean something."

She scooted over and burrowed into his chest.

"It's okay. I'm here," he soothed. He said other things softly into her hair.

He held on to her as the tears fell, staining her shirt.

She lifted her head, tears dripping. "You're doing everything right with her. Don't be too hard on yourself."

He thumbed away her tears.

"I've been so afraid of saying something wrong that I've been avoiding the topic. She stopped asking when her mother was coming back, stopped running to the door yelling, 'Mama!' every time UPS dropped off a package. And I just let it go."

"Sometimes people only come into our life for a moment and we'd like them to stay longer. And we want the world to know what a beautiful person they were, to know them like we do. But all we can do is honor their memory, their legacy. And be brave enough to live without them because I know in my heart that they wouldn't want us to be sad. Maribel's mother would want her to be happy. And you, too."

Dylan let those words sink in. Had he been punishing himself the past year because of his guilt over not being there for Lyndsey sooner?

He stared out the windshield for a while, thinking about everything Samantha had said.

Then his mind wound back to the present situation. "I just want you to know that I've heard everything you said. I have a lot of thinking to do." He paused. "First, we have a situation to take care of."

She nodded.

"My first instinct is to go to Alcorn directly, straight to the source."

"Roads keep leading to him, but he's the richest man in town. He has a lot of influence and it seems out of place that he'd do something like this."

"I'm not taking anything for granted when it comes to our families."

Sun was bright in the midmorning sky. Dylan noticed a glint from in between two houses across the street. "We need to—"

A crack sounded as a bullet whizzed past.

"GET DOWN," DYLAN commanded; his voice took a second to break through in her head.

Samantha dropped to the floorboard.

"Stay right there. You'll be safer."

Disbelief shrouded her. No way could any of this be real. Could it?

For all her panic, Dylan seemed amazingly calm.

"How'd they find us?"

"Someone might've been camping out at the gas station, waiting," he said, cutting a hard right.

One hand against the dash and the other against the seat, she crouched low and balanced herself.

Another round fired, from behind this time. The shooter was following them.

"Stay as low as you can while I lose them. Got it?"

"We can't be out in the open anymore. They'll kill us and then the people we love."

"If we keep you alive and out of sight, your father and Maribel will be safe."

Frustration peeled away her tough exterior.

Dylan made a few sharp turns, mixing lefts and rights. Suddenly, he stopped. "Get out."

Samantha pushed up. Her legs wobbled. Dammit. This was no time to let fear get the best of her. Toughness and strength defined the Turners. She commanded her legs to hold her. Surprisingly, they cooperated this time, and she sprung from the SUV.

"This way," Dylan said, his weapon drawn and ready.

Samantha ran in and out among the houses in the residential neighborhood until her thighs burned and her lungs clawed for oxygen.

Dylan finally stopped, barely breathing heavy. "We need alternate transportation."

"Where can we go? Neither of our houses is safe."

"I have an idea." He walked, surveying the area, until his gaze fell on a garage. "Wait here."

Samantha tried to hide behind the tree where Dylan had told her to stay put, praying the men wouldn't find her before he came back.

An electric car pulled up near the tree. She caught and held her breath, afraid to look to see who it was.

"Get in." Dylan's voice was a welcome relief.

With the way her body was beginning to burn, she didn't think she could make it any farther. She glanced down and saw blood on her shirt as she moved to the car. Panic stopped her. The blood was hers.

"Get in the back and stay down. Now," Dylan said firmly.

She did as he said, curling up across the backseat. She caught enough of a glimpse of him to see that he was wearing a ball cap.

A ripple of heat started in her stomach and was quickly

followed by a full-on wave of nausea. Light-headedness engulfed her like a flame. "I was shot."

"I know. You're going to be fine." Dylan's words came out strong and confident. There was an edge of anger there, too. "Can you see where you were hit?"

The numbness and the shock were wearing off; her left shoulder burned. "Yes."

"Stop the bleeding with this." Dylan passed back a shirt. "It's clean."

"Okay."

"We need to get to Brody and Rebecca's place."

"Won't they be watching our friends?" Samantha knew one thing was certain. If the guys got to her, then her father was as good as dead. Keeping herself out of sight was his only chance.

"Which is why we can't walk through the front door. I need to call Brody to let him know that we're coming."

"I've been thinking about something you said earlier. About my father's business."

Dylan nodded, eyes focused on the road ahead.

"I remember him being stressed a lot the first couple of years we came here. There were late-night discussions with Brent and Trevor as to whether Daddy had made the right choice in coming to Mason Ridge. Stevie was too young to weigh in. I blamed it on the changes in our lives, losing Mom..."

"But then Rebecca and Shane were kidnapped. Suddenly, Daddy was home every night. His drinking slowed down and then he quit altogether. His business turned around, too. He seemed sad but not as stressed, if that makes sense."

"It does."

"On the phone, Daddy said he knows what really happened that night. What if someone had bribed him to be quiet?"

"That was fifteen years ago. It would be impossible to trace the money now."

"Not with computers. Daddy keeps everything."

"So if we get into your dad's system, you think we'll figure out who's behind this?"

She was already nodding. "Except that every time we're out in the open, we seem to get shot at."

Dylan didn't argue that. He made a few more turns and then parked on the side of the road. Then he called Brody and asked for permission to come onto his land. Brody said he'd make arrangements for one of the guys to pick up Dylan's SUV. He turned to Samantha after ending the call. "We'll have to walk it from here."

Dylan opened her door and extended his hand.

She took it, noticing how strong and capable it felt. His hand was surprisingly soft, and she already knew how adept it was from the few times he'd touched her.

They hiked what felt like ten miles before Brody's barn came into view. Dylan led her into the back, and she could see all the way through to light at the other end. Both doors must have been open.

The barn was one big, impressively long hallway with light streaming in from both ends. The floors were made of concrete and there was hay strewn around everywhere. A dozen or so horse stalls with red metal gates flanked the left-hand side and there were a quarter as many doors to the right. She assumed they were supply rooms and offices.

Dylan opened the first, held on to her hand tightly and ushered her inside. "The horses must have been turned out in the paddock."

This room had to be Brody's office. Centering the

space was a large oak desk with a leather chair behind it. There was a matching sofa to her left. It was a rich dark tone and massive in size. Dylan guided her there and helped her ease down onto it.

There were no windows. It would be dark inside without the light on.

"Lie still." He placed a throw pillow behind her head.

On top of the desk was a white case with a red cross on it. A medical kit. Dylan retrieved it and instructed her to roll up the sleeve of her shirt.

She did.

The sofa dipped where he sat.

"No good. I can't see. Take it off." His words came out harshly. He clenched his jaw. "I can turn around if you want, but I'm going to need to see to fix you up anyway."

"It's okay. I have on a bra, which is a lot like wearing a swimsuit anyway, right?" She tried to sound convincing. Mostly, she needed to reassure herself that it was no big deal. Heat flushed her cheeks anyway as she eased out of her shirt with his help. Her left shoulder had been hit and it hurt when she moved. The wound itself was too bloody for her to really tell how bad it was, but the bleeding had stemmed.

Dylan grunted a few words under his breath when he saw it and she assumed they were the same words she was thinking. He pulled out the antiseptic wipes first, opened them and lined up a few on the sofa.

"This is going to sting. Let me know if it gets to be too much." He went to work cleaning her gunshot wound. His hands were assured and surprisingly gentle. She didn't want to know how he'd become so good at it, figuring he'd picked up the skill during his time in Afghanistan.

"How bad is it?" she said, not wanting to look anymore, wincing with pain.

"I'm sorry if I'm hurting you." His voice sounded pained.

"It could be a lot worse," she offered.

"The bleeding has stopped, so now we want to clean it up well to keep out infection," he said, tenderly blotting her wound with antibacterial pads before bandaging them.

When he was finished, his gaze drifted across her chest.

"Thank you for taking such good care of me," she said, ignoring the rapid rise of her pulse.

"That should do it." The words came out clipped.

She wondered if it had to do with the fact that she was lying there topless.

Chapter Nine

"All done," Dylan said as he forced his gaze away from her creamy skin. Her lacy bra didn't help matters. It had taken considerable discipline to avert his eyes from the soft curve of her full breasts peeking out over the top.

He told himself that it had been too long since he'd had sex, and that part was true. He didn't want to acknowledge how much it might not matter when it came to Samantha. Even so, when had there been time this past year to do anything but potty train Maribel? No wonder his body reacted every time he touched Samantha. She was a beautiful woman. He was a man with needs. If it had been that simple, he was pretty sure they'd have been in bed already, recent events aside. There was so much more to it than that. They had history. He knew that she secretly liked being silly and she prided herself on not being too much of a girlie girl. He figured that was a gift from growing up with three brothers. Her laugh filled him like spring air. She had a single dimple on her left cheek that came out only when she smiled real wide.

She'd asked to hold his hand earlier, to help deal with the pain, and he just now realized that his thumb was moving in small circles against her palm.

One look into her cobalt-blue eyes—eyes that had

darkened with the look he hadn't allowed himself to see in far too long—and his heart clutched.

If she hadn't been injured, he might have done something they'd both regret.

"You haven't slept. Do me a favor and try to close your eyes." He pulled his hand back, gathered up used supplies and tossed them into the garbage.

"I feel as though I should be doing something."

"We can't. Not until we know what their next move is," he said.

She seemed to carefully consider his words.

"You're right." She bit back a yawn as he turned off the light.

He hadn't wanted to admit just how freaked out he'd been when he saw that she'd been shot. He'd stayed calm for her benefit.

Dylan wouldn't survive losing her, too. *Where'd that come from?*

Thankfully, Samantha would be all right.

"Will you come over here?" Her sweet, sleepy voice wasn't helping with his arousal.

The room had just enough light for him to see big objects without being able to tell what they were. His own adrenaline was fading, leaving him fatigued.

He walked over and sat down. She took his hand. Hers was so small in comparison, so soft.

"Will you lie next to me?" she asked in that sexy, sleepy voice. "Just until I fall asleep?"

He settled onto his side, being sure to keep a safe distance between them, and realized she was trembling. A lightning bolt of anger sizzled down his spine.

"I'm right here," he whispered into her thick dark hair.

She wiggled until her back was flush with his chest, and she made a mewling sound as she snuggled against him. Her hips readjusted, causing her sweet round bottom to press against his swollen erection. His jeans were uncomfortably tight, so he shifted his position and she pressed into him farther. Blood pulsed thickly through his veins, and all he could think about this close was the lilac scent of her shampoo.

"Samantha."

"Yeah."

"You might not want to get so close to me."

"Sorry. I didn't mean to trap you." She made a pained noise as she moved.

"That's not the problem."

"No?"

"If those hips of yours press into me one more time, I can't be held responsible for my actions."

"Oh." It was dark in the room, but he could sense that she was smiling.

She shouldn't want anything to do with him. His life had been beyond messed up before the military. She swivcled her hips until she surely felt his straining erection.

"Samantha, I'm warning you not to do that."

"Now you're starting to sound like one of my brothers."

"I have nothing brotherly in mind to do to you right now. And if you weren't injured, we'd both be in serious trouble, because I don't make a habit of forcing myself on anyone."

"What makes you think I'd say no?"

That was the last thing he needed to hear.

"Are you intent on causing me more pain?"

"Sorry. No. Of course not." She wiggled again, this time to inch away from him. Big mistake.

He stopped her with a hand on her hip. He curled his fingers around her waist, which felt tiny in comparison to his hand, into her taut skin, and he knew he was falling down the rabbit hole. She was so close he could feel her breathing against his chest, her breath hitching with his touch, her body trembling underneath his fingers.

Neither said a word, but the moment felt insanely intimate.

After a few seconds passed, she finally said, "Is it wrong that I like how your body feels against mine?"

"No. But if we let this go any further, it would kill our friendship." Her shirt was still off and there was enough light for him to see her sexy silhouette. If trouble had a name, it would be Samantha.

His life had been ticking along fine before she waltzed in. Everything had finally made sense. He was meant to be Maribel's father. To this day, he figured he'd go to his grave wondering why Lyndsey had truly ditched him. Maybe she'd been smart enough to realize he wasn't good for her, for anyone.

And he'd surely kill his friendship with Samantha if he didn't maintain control, which was beyond difficult watching her breasts move up and down as she breathed.

Plus, he'd thought about those couple of kisses they'd shared way more than any man should.

Good grief, would he be calling his friends together for a glass of wine and to share feelings next?

How far did this out-of-control-emotions thing plan to go?

"You're probably right, but I can't help wondering what it would feel like if you ran your finger along here." She picked up his hand and ran his index finger along the waistline of her shorts.

She rolled onto her back, looked into his eyes and traced the lace on her bra next.

All he could do in that moment was dip his head and

claim her pink lips. He cupped her breast with his palm, and a jolt of need burst through him as her nipple beaded. His need for her, to be inside her, was so powerful it was a physical pain. And that scared him because he'd never felt that deep-seated need for anyone, not even Lyndsey. He'd never wanted to be inside anyone so much.

Her mouth moved under his, inviting him to explore. He slid his tongue between her lips and she opened her mouth to give him better access.

With her hands tunneling in his hair, roaming his chest, his skin burned with sexual energy.

All that was between his hand and her breast was a thin piece of lace. He traced down her stomach, lowering his hand until he was on her sex.

She moaned and bit his bottom lip, drawing it out between her teeth.

His desire for her was almost a savage force inside him now.

"Samantha." He pulled back long enough to look into her eyes, needing to know she wanted this as much as he did, because much more and he'd be over the tipping point, no turning back. Her eyes were dark and glittery, her face flushed, her lips pink and swollen from kissing. She was the most incredibly sexy woman…

And it was clear she wanted exactly the same thing he did—mind-numbing, mind-blowing sex.

Dylan took in a sharp breath.

There was one more thing he wanted. And that darn thing would stop him from getting the others.

He'd promised himself that the next time he had sex, it would be with someone he had strong feelings for. He didn't want to say love, because, frankly, love was complicated as hell.

"I let this go too far," he said, pushing off the sofa and

into a sitting position. His punishment pulsed painfully against his zipper.

"Oh. You don't like me enough?" He hated the sound of embarrassment in her voice.

"I like you just fine. You're freakin' beautiful. And that body." He took in another sharp breath.

"Then, I'm confused. You want me, right?"

"Yeah."

"And I want this to happen, too."

"It would seem so."

"Then, what's the problem?"

He didn't want to tell her that he didn't have strong enough feelings for her. His were strong. And confusing as all hell. But mostly a complication he couldn't afford right now. Introducing another change in Maribel's life when he'd just given her some stability was out of the question. "It's Bel."

She gave him a confused look.

"If things were different, then maybe we could take our time, date and see where this goes. But that's not a priority for me right now and, frankly, I don't have time for it to be."

His words had the effect of a slap in the face. He didn't enjoy being harsh, but he'd said all of that more for him than her.

She covered herself with her shirt, turned on her side and then did what every woman he'd ever known had done to him when he'd said the wrong thing. Gave him the silent treatment.

HUMILIATION WAS A PYTHON wrapped around Samantha, squeezing. Not only had she basically just thrown herself at one of her oldest friends, but she'd been rejected by him. Painfully. And if her shoulder didn't hurt so much, she'd have tossed and turned on this sofa or gotten up and stormed out. But it did. And she couldn't move any more than she could allow herself to cry. *Mortified* didn't begin to cover her embarrassment. If there'd been a crack big enough in the wall, she'd have slipped through it. While she was at it, why not ask for a tiny bottle or a looking glass? Her life made about as much sense. Then again, if she was really having her wishes granted, she should definitely aim for something higher, like forgetting any of this had ever happened. Or getting her father out of trouble. Or, better yet, saving her father and Dylan's little girl.

Frustration burned through her like chunks of a comet spiraling toward Earth.

They had no idea who they were really chasing and time was running out.

She strained to listen to Dylan, who was talking quietly into his cell phone on the other side of the room. Her eyes had adjusted to the dark. He was bent forward, his arms resting on his knees, being too quiet for her to be able to hear what he was saying. Most likely because he didn't want to interrupt her while she was supposed to be sleeping.

Slowly, she eased onto her back. The pain in her shoulder had already started thumping, and she could feel it worsen with every beat of her heart.

He ended the call and crossed the room, setting himself up to pace. He glanced down, looking as if his anger was barely contained, and his gaze stopped on her. She could've sworn his tongue slicked across his lips.

At his full height, he was imposing, to say the least, especially with his arms folded across his broad chest. And, as much as she didn't want to think about it, he was incredibly sexy.

"Who were you talking to?"

"Jorge. He sent me photos of Alcorn's security team and I didn't see our guys."

"Which means they don't work for him."

"They might be off the books, but we can't link them." He stalked to one end of the room and back.

"Have you figured out what they want us to do next?"

"You're injured and need to rest." Surely he wasn't saying what she thought.

"Oh, no. You're not leaving me here while you go out there." She motioned toward outside.

His face was carved in stone. "They have my daughter. And I'm running out of time."

"We are. Or don't you do 'we'?" She shouldn't have gone there but she did anyway. His earlier rejection still stung.

She geared up, expecting a fight. Instead, he softened his stance and there was a quirky little smirk settled into the corners of his mouth. *Damn.* Even when she wanted to throttle him, he was being sexy.

"You got me there. But that doesn't change the fact that you've been shot. You lost blood today and you have to take that seriously. You're safe here for the time being, and that's the best gift you can give to your father and Maribel. They don't want me. They want *you*. Even if they catch me, I'm not the target. *You are*."

Didn't those words send a chill up Samantha's spine?

"I see your point but I have a question. Where does that leave me? You're all I have right now. Anything happens to you and I might as well walk into the center of Main Street and take a seat. They'll get to me. You're the only thing keeping me safe." As much as it scared and angered her to admit it, she needed him. And a traitorous piece of her heart actually didn't mind depending on someone else. And that was just ridiculous, because she'd fought for her independence from her three older brothers for how long?

What was so different about Dylan that depending on him didn't make her feel as if she was being less than in some way?

His hands came up, palms out, in the universal sign of surrender. "I want you with me. Believe me. That's the only way I can be guaranteed of your safety. Your injury is making bringing you with me that much more diffi- cult. We might end up in a situation where we have to be able to run and get away quickly. I don't know what I'll be facing but I have to investigate those woods."

She appreciated that he didn't point out that she'd be slowing him down, even if that was the writing on the wall. He would be right. She would hold him back. The men she and Dylan were up against seemed to anticipate her movements. They had resources. And they seemed to be right there, waiting, no matter which way she and Dylan turned.

And that was definitely not good.

"I'll have Brody check in on you. He doesn't nor- mally spend much time in his office, so he's trying not to change his behavior in front of his staff. It's best if we can fly under the radar as much as possible right now. Rebecca said she'd figure out a way to send food in. She wishes we'd stay in the house but she understands that it's too risky."

"I don't want to put anyone else in harm's way. There's already enough on the line here as it is." She didn't want to think about what those men might be doing to her fa- ther.

"They won't kill him. Not as long as you're out here and they believe you know the truth." Dylan didn't say that they wouldn't torture her father, beat him trying to get information out of him. The thought left acid churning in her stomach. Bile rose to her throat, burning her esophagus.

"Whatever he might've done or been involved in, he's not a bad person."

"I know."

She looked up at him, grateful. An emotion she couldn't quite put her finger on crossed behind his eyes.

"Speaking of which, we need to get your father's computer information to my contact. He might be able to access it remotely and quite possibly give us a name to work with." Dylan held up his phone.

"Right. Let's see what he can dig up."

Jorge, true to form, picked up on the second ring.

"I need you to take a peek into a computer for me," Dylan said into the line. "And there's someone I'd like you to talk to."

After relaying her name, Dylan passed the cell toward her.

Samantha took the offering and said, "Hello."

"Nice to meet you. Well, sort of. What do you have for me?" Jorge asked.

"I can give you file names and passwords. How you'll get into the system, I have no idea."

"Don't figure you have an IP address for me?"

"That would be a no."

"You have a website or social media page?"

"Yeah. Both."

"Give me the company name and I'll work from there." That was all he needed to access data files? That was scary, she thought as she rattled off the information.

"Cool. Tell Snap-trap to stay put. Let him know that I'll call back in a few minutes."

"Snap-trap?" She glanced at Dylan, who was shaking his lowered head.

"Oh, yeah. Crud. I'm pretty sure that'll get me in trouble. I mean that big ugly guy standing next to you."

She thanked Jorge and ended the call with an eyebrow cocked toward Dylan. "You plan on explaining that one?"

"You don't want to know what it means."

"I think I do, actually. How on earth did you pick up the name Snap-trap?"

Had his cheeks just flushed red-hot? It was about time he was embarrassed instead of her.

"I'd tell you but I took an oath never to discuss it. And he wasn't supposed to, either."

She stood so she could look him in the eyes. Thankfully, only her shoulder hurt and not her legs. "I have one word for you."

"Really?" He crossed his arms over his chest. "Do you care to impart your...wisdom?"

"I sure do."

"Today?"

"Fine. Here goes. My word for you is...*chicken*."

Chapter Ten

Chicken? Dylan had half a mind to show her what was really on his. If he did, there'd be no going back, because it involved the two of them being naked on that couch. And he couldn't go there right now, no matter how much his body battled him.

"I have a word for you, too," he said.

"I'm not so sure I want to hear this." Her tongue darted across her lips, and he thought about how good she tasted, how he liked the way they fit when their bodies were molded together.

Against his better judgment, he wrapped his arm around her waist and pulled her toward him until her body was flush with his. He was tempting his self-control with the move but there were times when he just had to say to hell with it.

"Beautiful. Sexy. Intelligent."

"That's three words," she said against his mouth.

"I never was good at following rules." He stood his ground. For the moment, logical thought ruled. If he stayed much longer, he couldn't be certain he wouldn't change his mind. And that was another reason he wanted to break off on his own. He needed to clear his thoughts. Being this close to her was doing crazy things to his normally practical head.

"You lose." With that, she delved her tongue inside his mouth. His body tensed, all his muscles locking up at the same time, and he decided not to fight it. Instead, he placed his hand on the back of her neck, curling his fingers around the base, and tilted her head.

Dylan had had wild sex in the past but nothing that compared to the heat in this kiss.

When he gathered enough willpower to pull back, he pressed his forehead to hers. "*Damn*. Keep that up and you're going to destroy me."

He'd never believed in kisses that made a person go weak at the knees until right then.

His cell buzzed.

Dylan took a sharp breath. He needed to put a little space between him and Samantha. He liked how she fit him a little too much for either his or her own good.

A glance at the screen said it was Jorge. He showed it to her and then answered.

"I got interesting information for you, bro."

"Hit me with it." Dylan held the phone so that Samantha could hear.

"The corporation that owns the property for your drop is the same one that sent considerable funds to her father's company about fifteen years ago. They've been making deposits ever since."

Samantha sank down to her knees and folded forward. Dylan guided her to the couch.

"You got any idea who's behind that company?"

"Not yet. I'm still digging, though."

"Thanks, man. I appreciate it."

"You might not be thanking me when I send you my invoice this month." Jorge laughed.

Dylan ended the call. Samantha sat there looking lost and alone, in fierce contrast to the woman who'd been in his arms moments ago. A little piece of the armor guarding his heart cracked.

"We'll get to the bottom of this."

"You know what this says, right?"

"It doesn't necessarily mean—"

"What? That my dad is blackmailing someone? I think we're both pretty clear on what's happening."

It certainly explained why he had the money to send four kids to college after cashing out their life savings to move to Mason Ridge. Dylan hadn't really thought about it before, but her father had sure pulled off a miracle. Bringing up kids was expensive. He knew that firsthand.

There weren't exactly long lines out the door of the hardware store. Purchases were small. Her dad would've had to sell a lot of nails to pull off raising four kids. Not that they were rich by any means. But sending four kids to four-year colleges was no small feat these days.

Then again, Samantha had gone on athletic scholarship.

"Did you or your brothers take out college loans?"

"Nope. None of us. Most of mine was paid for by my scholarship, but he paid for the boys."

"I know how this looks, but we don't want to convict him without hearing his side of the story."

"You're being awfully generous to a man who is most likely a criminal."

"Nope." He leaned back on his heels. "I'm covering all the bases. Your father blackmailing someone is just one angle out of a possible half dozen scenarios."

"You have other ideas?"

"Someone could have been paying him to stay quiet, threatening him. We keep circling back to Alcorn, and he has the money to silence pretty much anyone. Your dad might've decided to break the deal, and so Alcorn came after him. And when he couldn't get to him, he tried to snatch you."

"That explains a lot. You might be right and I want to believe it. Even so, that's still breaking the law."

"Maybe he didn't feel as if he had a choice. A desperate parent would go to any lengths for their children." Dylan had no doubt he'd kill for Maribel if push came to shove. Other than that, he couldn't see himself breaking the law, but then, he hadn't been in a position where he'd needed to. He didn't rule anything out.

She stared at him for a long moment. "I can see that you'd do anything for your daughter."

"Without a doubt. A parent's love is a powerful thing."

Her chest deflated and she winced at the motion, glancing toward her sore shoulder.

"I can give you something for the pain. You don't have to be a hero." He made a move toward the first-aid kit.

She nodded.

Good. Watching her suffer when he knew he could help was worse than him being the one to take a bullet. There was already so much pain he couldn't take from her. At least he could give her a pair of ibuprofen and help her shoulder. Dylan located a bottle of water and brought the pain relievers to her.

She dry swallowed them, squeezed off the plastic cap and then took a good drink.

He had to fight the urge to take her into his arms again. He'd just be playing with fire. Dylan needed space. His fingers curled and released a few times, and that was better than letting them do what they wanted. If they had their way, they'd be tunneled into her dark mane while he kissed her again.

And that would be a mistake.

"Think you can rest?" he asked.

"Probably not but it never hurts to try."

"Good. Close your eyes and by the time you open them again, I should be back." Dylan had no plans to be a liar. He pressed a kiss to her forehead.

Dylan packed his duffel with a protein bar and water and then listened at the door for a solid twenty minutes before making a move. He slipped out of the office and the barn and into the nearby woods without drawing attention to himself.

Hiking to the abandoned car took half an hour on his own. He made much better time that way. Too bad he couldn't use the small sedan. There'd be a stolen-vehicle report by now. Last thing he needed was to be picked up and detained.

Normally, he liked being on his own, but his thoughts bounced back and forth between Maribel and Samantha, and worry was a wildfire unleashed inside him, engulfing him. He told himself that this was exactly what it would be like to have a woman in his life permanently. His attention would be divided. He'd always be battling between needing to protect Maribel and be both mother and father to her and trying to spend enough time with someone new to develop a relationship.

Maribel deserved better. She was his priority, *had* to be his main concern. Always. She'd already lost so much.

Otherwise, Samantha would have been exactly the type of woman he could see himself asking out, spending some time getting to know better.

He almost laughed out loud. He'd known Samantha since fifth grade. He'd kissed her more times than he'd intended to in the past twenty-four hours, and his body already had her imprint. How much better did he need to *know* someone in order to go on a date?

Luckily, Brody's place wasn't too far from Mason

Ridge Lake. Dylan slipped through the woods rather than taking a main road. He could hike there in an hour at this pace. This time, he fully intended to surprise the bastard who'd taken his Maribel instead of being on the receiving end of the surprise again. His plan was to come from behind the lake, gain a perspective and then secure the target.

He figured the item was near the shed that Rebecca and Shane had been taken to when they'd been kidnapped, a sick reminder that this guy was still in control.

Not for long.

Dylan held on to those three words as he pushed through the underbrush, thankful he was wearing jeans. At least he had something to cover his ankles. His arms were getting torn up by the branches thanks to short sleeves.

For the past hour, he'd been able to think about only two things: Maribel and Samantha.

It would be dark in a few hours and he hated the thought that his baby would sleep away from her bed another night. Fury tore through him.

No. Maribel would sleep at home in her own room, wearing her own pajamas by the time the sun rose on a new day. He repeated the mantra over and over in his head.

He pulled his binoculars out of his pack and crouched low. Patience won fights. Fights won battles. Battles won wars.

And he had a deep freakin' well.

Dylan hadn't counted how many hours had passed since he'd taken his position. Three guys, together, came and went at different points during his stay. They were checking back regularly, trying to be stealthy but making a ton of noise to his trained ear. There was always something with civilians that made it easy to track them. He'd followed them to their vehicle once, his heart pounding by the time he reached the Ford F-150, thinking they might have brought her with them. Maribel had not been inside.

The guys left again and Dylan decided to make his move. At a minimum, he had half an hour to find the doll. None of the guys hung back, so it was now or never.

SAMANTHA HAD BEEN pacing for hours when a soft knock at the door came. Her nerves were already set to burning embers, so she jumped at the noise. No way would Dylan knock, and she didn't want to give away the fact they were staying in the barn should this be a worker looking for Brody. She scooted around the side of the desk, out of view, and searched for a weapon just in case. Samantha had no intention of being caught off guard ever again. She might startle at noises for the rest of her life but she would never be jumped again.

The door slowly opened as she gripped a fire extinguisher and crouched low. Anyone who got close was about to be clobbered.

"Samantha?" Rebccca whispered. The door closed softly.

"Right here." Samantha let out the breath she'd been holding on a small sigh and stood. She glanced at the fire extinguisher in her hand at the same time Rebecca did. "Sorry. It's been a rough few days."

"Believe me. I know." Rebecca, white-knuckling a food container, lightened her grip as she walked over to Samantha and hugged her.

"I'm so sorry for everything you've gone through." And Samantha meant every word. Guilt washed over her as she embraced her friend. If her father really had known what had happened that night all those years ago, as he claimed, then he could've helped find Shane. Losing him had destroyed the Hughes family, the town. Samantha didn't want to admit to her friend what she suspected about her father. And yet not telling Rebecca felt like a whole different kind of betrayal.

"We found him. He's alive. That's all that really matters," Rebecca said.

"But your family…"

"My parents would've split up eventually. I've come to realize that now. Probably better to have figured it out years ago so they could get on with their lives," Rebecca said thoughtfully. "I don't know if I can ever truly forgive Thomas Kramer for what he did—don't get me wrong. Losing Shane was the hardest thing I've ever been through, and I never want to go through that again. I still can't even think of having children of my own yet. But I also don't want to walk around with a chip on my shoulder."

"Makes it feel as though they've won in a weird way, doesn't it?" Samantha hated that feeling. She wanted to tell Rebecca the person truly responsible might be Charles Alcorn. She couldn't. Not yet. Not until they had evidence.

"Exactly. Nobody has time for that." Rebecca smiled.

Maybe Samantha could forgive her father. She'd done it before when he was drinking. Not that being a drunk was a good excuse or gave him a free pass, but she knew he never would've made the decision to cover up a kidnapping if he'd been sober. If that was in fact what he'd done.

He'd been part of the search team. Had all that been for show?

Chapter Eleven

Dylan stretched his sore legs to work out a cramp. He'd learned to slip through worse terrain unnoticed during his tour, and the few scrapes he'd collected on his arms weren't anything more than a small nuisance. Nothing a little antibiotic ointment couldn't fix.

The shed where Rebecca had been taken when she'd been kidnapped had long since been destroyed. Dylan stood on the same ground now. A cold chill tickled his spine.

Even in summer there were dead leaves scattered on the ground.

These activities being tied to a corporation gave him the impression this might be one helluva sophisticated child-selling operation. That was the only thing that made sense. Had more kids been taken in other counties across Texas? Across the country?

A dummy corporation with lots of money was in the game. People hid behind overseas accounts because they were committing crimes. Child slavery. Sex trade. Those were two realistic options. Shane was older. He hadn't been sold or hurt. Kramer had raised him as his own son. After he left for the military, Kramer had taken another boy, Jason, who'd been returned to his family after a year.

There was clearly a bigger story. Otherwise, everything would've died with Kramer in the car crash that had taken his life.

Mr. Turner was the only one who knew what that story was, and quite possibly the only one who could prove Charles Alcorn was involved.

There was nothing at the site, no clues.

A thought hit him. Those jerks patrolling the area might know something. And Dylan had ways of making people talk.

He retraced his steps, moving stealthily through the trees.

One of the guys was leaning against the tailgate of the pickup. Another was talking— he was nearby, but Dylan couldn't get a visual from his vantage point to the left of the Ford. He'd need to get closer.

There were three men—he already knew that—and Dylan could be certain he knew the location of two.

He had two choices. He could attack and then force one of them to talk. Three against one wasn't bad odds against civilians. He'd sized them up earlier. Two were a little smaller than him. One was similar in size. That guy might present a problem. All three together, considering each one carried a weapon, might be difficult to take down. If he could isolate them, he'd have a better chance at walking out of this alive and, better yet, with the information he was looking for.

His other choice?

He could wait it out until they left. Make himself a passenger in the bed of the truck and let them lead him to whoever was behind this. What if they made contact only via the phone?

Dylan couldn't be certain they would go to the person in charge. In fact, that would be a stupid move, when he really thought about it. The most likely scenario was that they were low in the pecking order. They wouldn't have direct contact with the boss.

Recognition dawned. These were the same guys from the pics on Mr. Turner's phone.

The third guy, the big bearded one, came into view. Unfortunately, he stepped out from behind a tree five feet away from Dylan, and the guy's eyes were locked onto his target—Dylan.

Fighting had just made top priority.

Dylan rolled back onto his shoulders and then popped to his feet. Using momentum, he brought his elbow down on Bearded's face. The crack was so loud it echoed. Bearded, blood shooting out of his nose, already had Dylan in a bear hug.

There'd be no wiggling out of the guy's viselike grip.

"Hey, guys. We have company," Bearded yelled toward the truck.

Dylan couldn't reach the gun tucked into his waistband, either. Well, hell's bells, this wasn't how he'd planned for this little exchange to go. He needed to even the score.

He reared back and then head-butted Bearded.

More blood splattered on his T-shirt. Wouldn't be salvageable once this was over. No amount of bleach could get it out.

At least his maneuver loosened Bearded's grip enough for Dylan to drop down and roll away. He came up with his Glock pointed at Bearded.

The other two jerks were already rushing over.

"Stop or I'll shoot your friend here," Dylan said.

"Hold on there, country boy. We didn't ask for trouble," one of the guys said, hands up in surrender.

"Then, you won't mind if I leave." Dylan took a step back. If he could gain a few steps of advantage, he had no doubt he could outrun these guys. Once safely in the trees, it'd be hard for them to get a clean shot. He could get away and get back to Samantha.

He took another step backward as he evaluated his options. At this distance, he could spin and dart through the trees with certainty the men wouldn't be able to catch him.

Or there was another idea worth considering...

"I'm going to put my hands up and step toward you guys," Dylan said as he did what he said—took a step toward the men.

Bearded's slack-jawed expression outlined his shock. He was right, though. No one in his right mind would give up when he had the advantage.

Dylan placed his gun on the ground, kicked it away from him and then rose to an athletic stance, feet wide with arms crossed. "So, fellas, where are we headed next?"

"I'M JUST GLAD you're all right," Rebecca said as she thrust the Tupperware toward Samantha.

Even though whatever it was smelled amazing, she didn't think she could take a bite until Dylan came back.

"Thank you for helping us." Samantha opened the container and found chicken and mushroom risotto. She grabbed the fork.

"He's pretty special. Dylan. And his daughter is the most adorable thing I've ever seen," Rebecca said, sitting next to Samantha on the couch.

She moved a piece of chicken around in her bowl.

"You can eat that later if you want. It won't hurt my feelings," Rebecca said, smiling. "There's a small fridge behind the desk. I totally understand if you want to wait for Dylan."

"It looks amazing. I don't know what's wrong with me," Samantha said.

"You're worried. Like I said, Dylan is a remarkable person." Rebecca smiled and something lit up behind her eyes.

Samantha chose to ignore the comment. Her friend was absolutely right. But Dylan had no intention of allowing anyone else into his life, and she understood that on some level. Her father had closed up to relationships after her mother had died. Once he'd sobered up, he'd thrown all his energy into being a good dad. If he couldn't be at one of her volleyball games, he'd made sure one of her brothers could. He'd never raised his voice or given her pointers while he was watching from the stands. All he'd ever given was a few words of encouragement, lots of smiles and support.

Had he done all that because of a guilty conscience? Tried to make up for his greatest sin by being the perfect father to her? If so, that would make him almost as bad as the criminals who'd committed the crime all those years ago.

No. He's a good man.

There had to have been extenuating circumstances for him to hide the truth about what happened that night. He was a father and knew what it was like to lose someone, and he wouldn't want to put another family through the sorrow his family had endured in losing Samantha's mother.

She wanted her father home more than anything. And not just to figure out what the heck was going on, although she wanted to know that, too. He was getting older, and he'd seemed frail to her lately. She feared his heart wouldn't be able to take whatever these guys did to him.

Maybe his memories haunted him? And that was why he wanted to come clean now?

"How is Shane?" Samantha asked.

"Good. He's overseas, so we haven't had a chance to speak to him that much. He's so grown now." Rebecca had a wistful look in her eyes.

"Do you talk about what happened?"

"Not really. His calls are limited while he's deployed. We're just happy to know he's healthy. We've promised to catch up when he has a little time to spend with us."

"And your mom? How's she doing?"

"Better, actually. She finally agreed to take the medicine the doctor's been trying to get her to take for months and it seems to be helping. She's still weak but improving. I know she won't be around forever, but it feels good to be able to give her son back to her before she…" Rebecca focused her gaze on her shoelaces and twisted her hands.

"I'm so grateful that everything worked out." Samantha hated lying to her friend, especially since Rebecca had been through so much already. And to think her dad had been somehow involved…

"We've spent so much time in the past." Rebecca stretched her legs out in front of her. "Time to switch gears, you know? Besides, what can be gained by going back now? We have the rest of our lives to get reacquainted and it feels good to have my family back. Brody and I are starting to plan the wedding, and you have to be there."

"I can't wait." Samantha managed a smile. It faded almost immediately. "Dylan should have returned already. I have a bad feeling about this."

Rebecca put her arm around Samantha's shoulder, careful not to touch the gauze. "He's strong and he knows what's at stake. He'll walk through that door any minute."

"I hope you're right." She closed the Tupperware lid.

"You don't have to talk about it if you don't want to, but are you okay?" Rebecca asked.

How did Samantha answer that truthfully?

"When this ordeal is over, I will be." She didn't add *if I'm still alive*. Then there was her father to think about…

Or the fact that she'd never be able to forgive herself if anything happened to Maribel or Dylan.

"Can I ask a question?" Samantha needed to know more about Dylan.

"Anything."

"How did Maribel's mother fit into the picture?"

"She kept her pregnancy a secret, which tells me she didn't really know Dylan very well."

"For as much as he used to talk about never having kids, he would never walk away from his child," Samantha agreed. "How did he find out about her sickness?"

"Dylan hasn't said much to me. I don't think he talks about it to anyone, not even Brody, and you know how close the guys are."

Samantha nodded.

"Brody and Dylan lost touch during Dylan's tour. One day, Brody gets this call out of the blue asking him to come to New Mexico. He took off that day not knowing what he was going to find, only that it wasn't good based on the sound of Dylan's voice.

"Dylan was holed up in a motel room, a mess. Brody asked what was wrong but Dylan was too inside himself to speak. He just held up a bottle of tequila, so Brody took it and drank with him. The next morning, Dylan was up by dawn. Brody was hungover and fuzzy but he hopped out of bed, showered. Next thing he knew, he dressed, followed Dylan to the car and then the two of them rode in silence to a funeral."

It wasn't the same thing, but she remembered the silent car ride to her own mother's funeral. Everyone had been too overwrought with emotion, too spent, to speak. Samantha hurt from the inside out for Dylan.

"When my mother passed away, it was tough. I can't imagine losing a spouse."

"If anything happened to Brody, I'd be lost," Rebecca said wistfully. "We could never be sure if Dylan and Lyndsey were married. In fact, I don't think they were. He never talks about it, though."

"Brody never mentioned anything about going to a wedding?" Samantha asked.

"No. You know Dylan, though. He's always been private. He doesn't let anyone in."

"True." Samantha could attest to that. She'd been close a few times, but each time it was as if a door had been slammed in her face. When she really thought about it, he'd always been like that. He was the first person to jump in if a friend was in need but she couldn't remember a time when he'd asked for help. And he could be trusted with secrets. "Remember that time when we all decided it would be a good idea to go swimming in the lake after school?"

"What was that? Fifth grade?" Rebecca asked thoughtfully.

"Yeah, it was. I'd just moved here and someone, I can't even remember who now, thought it would be a good idea to welcome me by taking me to the lake."

"Which was strictly forbidden without an adult present, but what did we know?"

"We came running back, laughing, soaking wet, the whole lot of us, and Ryan's dad stopped us in the street."

"He had such a bad home life. We knew it wasn't good

to see his father." Rebecca's eyes grew wide as if they were reliving the episode.

"His dad was so angry we all froze. Not Dylan. He stepped up and said we were walking home cutting across the McGills' yard when the sprinklers came on."

"I do remember that. We all smelled like lake water, so Dylan stayed in between Ryan and his father." Rebecca smiled. "He most likely saved Ryan from another beating."

"Then he hosed us all down to get the lake-water smell out of our clothes. He thought of just about everything." She didn't say why he'd learned to be so diligent. His grandmother had been kind enough to take him in, but she had been a spare-the-rod-spoil-the-child type. And that was probably half the reason her daughter, Dylan's mother, had taken off and not returned. Growing up in a house with an iron fist tended to create rebellion.

"This group has been through a lot together," Rebecca said. "You guys were a lifesaver for me, which is why I'd like to be there for you. Are you sure you don't want to talk about whatever's going on? I know you, and there's something you're not telling me. There's nothing you could've done that can't be fixed."

Didn't that make shards of guilt pelt Samantha's skin like a needle shower? What if her father could've saved Rebecca all that heartache but didn't? Everything inside Samantha wanted to come clean with her friend and tell her everything. The right words didn't come, so she said, "No one's perfect, including me, but I didn't do anything illegal. My situation is…complicated. It involves more than me and I hope you can understand that I need to protect the other person right now even if that means keeping secrets from my friends."

"Just know that we're here for you, no matter what."

Rebecca nodded her understanding, but her eyebrow lifted so slightly that Samantha thought she might've imagined it.

She'd told the truth. Even though she felt like the biggest liar, she had to protect her father. He owed them an explanation. A piece of her couldn't think that he'd knowingly done anything illegal.

Samantha hated secrets.

If her father hadn't kept his, none of this would have been happening right now.

Oh, Daddy, what have you gotten us into?

"I better get back to the house," Rebecca said, looking Samantha in the eye. "You gonna be okay?"

"Yeah. Thank you for dinner. And everything else." Samantha hugged her friend.

For now, all that mattered was bringing her father home alive. Dylan and his daughter, too, for that matter. Samantha glanced at the clock. It was nine thirty. He'd been gone four hours and twenty-seven minutes.

Where was he?

"No problem. If you need anything, use the phone in here to call the house. It's just me and Brody, so one of us will answer." Rebecca rose and started toward the door. She stopped short. "And be careful."

"Of course I will."

"Not just with what's going on. I'm talking about with Dylan."

Had Rebecca picked up on the fact that Samantha had feelings for Dylan? Had she been *that* transparent?

"Don't worry. We're good. It's nice to have a friend who has your back," she managed to get out, hoping the emphasis on friendship would throw Rebecca off the trail. Samantha wasn't sure why she wanted to keep her feelings for Dylan private, but she knew that telling everyone wouldn't change the fact that a relationship between them wasn't going to happen.

Samantha sat quietly for a long while after the door closed. She tried to get food down, remembering what Dylan had said about how important it was to keep nourished. It was no use. She couldn't manage more than a couple of bites.

She'd been pacing for a solid hour when she decided to venture outside, knowing full well she'd face his wrath if he caught her.

It didn't matter. The thought of him lying in a ditch somewhere, bleeding out, spurred her to make the decision. She'd deal with the consequences of her actions when she had to.

Chapter Twelve

Dylan was sure he'd been hit by a semi. That was the only logical explanation for the degree to which his head pounded, other than Bearded, of course, who'd gone to town with the butt of his gun on Dylan's face. *That's gonna leave a mark.*

He had to be amused. He'd had no plans to fight back. All he'd done was protect his head and vital organs as best he could.

The toe of Bearded's boot could have done a lot of damage to Dylan's spleen or any number of other essential organs. And after Dylan had split the guy's nose, revenge was fresh on Bearded's mind.

Dylan wanted the guys to take him with them, hazarding it was his best chance to get answers or get closer to Maribel. He'd made a promise to himself that she'd sleep in her own bed before first light, and he had every intention of following through on that commitment. He didn't care how determined these guys seemed to be that this would go down another way.

There'd most likely be more beatings tonight. They'd want to try to scare him to find out if he knew where Samantha was hiding. And he'd act the part.

And then when he was ready to walk out the front

door with his Maribel, he had every intention of doing just that, too.

Timing and discipline were two of Dylan's best virtues.

For now, he needed information, so he'd let the bad guys think they'd won. He'd played the role of the broken victim, needing to know more. His fear was that this operation was bigger than anyone had imagined. Texas was the perfect place to move "product." And that meant innocent kids. His hands involuntarily fisted and he realized his nails were digging into his flesh. Not good to let them get at him emotionally.

Dylan needed to remain calm and cool, ready to play his part when they came back to teach him another "lesson." And they would come back. But first he needed to survey his surroundings. They most likely wouldn't take him straight to the boss, whom he fully expected to be Charles Alcorn.

That would be a stupid move.

However, they might take him to a warehouse on the outskirts of town. He blinked his eyes open, squinting through the burn. He tried to move his arms, but they were bound behind his back at the wrists. Had they subdued him enough to throw him into something... A locked room? Maybe an office?

This was not the time to be thinking about the feel of Samantha's body against his, her silky skin or the lilac smell of her hair. He especially shouldn't be thinking about those intelligent dark eyes staring into his. Or the sexy way her lips parted for his.

Distractions had no business on a mission.

Footsteps echoed from down the hall.

Dylan wiggled around on his side. He blinked to try to get his eyes adjusted to the darkness.

His legs were loosely bound and he was on top of some kind of wooden table. He rolled onto his back, ignoring the piercing pain screaming between his shoulder blades, and looked up. A single bulb hung from a socket. There were plastic-looking panels on the ceiling. When it was light outside, sun would stream through the half wall of windows. How many hours had he been knocked out?

There was one thing this place would be good for. *Torture.*

Dylan thought about all the scenarios that could possibly go down. He visualized his movements in each, prepping for the very real possibility he'd be fighting all three men or more.

He wanted time to investigate the building, figure out if this was a holding cell for their product. He hadn't heard a noise in the few minutes he'd been conscious, and that led him to believe he might be the only one there.

As he tried to finagle his arms free, something stirred down the hall. He stopped and listened carefully.

The sound moving toward him was boot on concrete. It would be Bearded or one of the other guys. Maybe all three.

Dylan's senses were dulled by the ache splitting his head into two pieces. Damn. If only he had time, he'd be more than happy to return the favor to Bearded. A few punches in the gut should do the trick. It wasn't as though the guys were in shape. Dylan was almost embarrassed about letting the guys get the drop on him. Their skills weren't exactly what he was used to coming up against in the military. But then, that had played to his advantage, so he'd swallowed his pride and let them think they had him.

Getting Maribel back was the goal.

That was the only thing that mattered.

He imagined gently placing his sleepy girl into her bed, tucking her under the covers and retreating to the corner to watch her sleep. When he got her back, he had no plans to let her out of his sight again.

The metal door creaked and groaned as it opened. No doubt whoever was there intended to torture Dylan. He could only wonder what they would use. Waterboarding? Nah. That was probably too sophisticated for these small-time criminals.

The ceiling was high, but they could still manage to throw a rope around the exposed beam and tie him up, beat him with a pipe or other metal object, use pliers to pull his fingernails or use wire cutters on him. They could shoot his feet so he couldn't try to run, blindfold him and perform the ever-popular mock execution. That generally got the blood pumping.

Either way, they wouldn't be able to get him to tell them where Samantha was hiding.

"Sit up." The deep-boom voice belonged to Bearded.

"I'm a little tied up at the moment." Dylan quirked a smile as he raised his head.

His smart-alecky retort was rewarded with a punch to his face. His head popped back but he kept on smirking.

"That all you got?" Dylan turned his head to the side and spit blood. All he needed to do was keep them off balance just a little. Have them thinking about how much they hated him rather than wondering why he'd give up so easily in the first place. He moved his jaw from side to side, his hands still bound behind his back as he tried to work the bindings. He wasn't getting anywhere on freeing himself. Rolling to the side earlier, he'd realized that they'd taken his cell. That was a bugger.

Bearded reared his balled fist back to take another

swing, but one of the other guys grabbed him at the elbow.

"Save it for later. He's just being a jerk. We've been told what to do with him."

That sounded ominous.

The other guy who had been silently standing near Bearded had moved behind Dylan.

What the heck was he up to?

Dylan coiled into a tight ball to protect his organs. There wasn't much he could do about his head being exposed. But he could salvage other important things. He hadn't been able to work the binding—what he figured was duct tape—around his wrists enough to free himself. With his knees at his chin, he could buck and take out at least one of them, maybe two.

As he waited for the right moment to strike, he was suddenly hauled up to a sitting position from behind. Something was shoved over his head, plunging him into complete blackness again. A canvas bag? The next thing he knew, there was pressure against his larynx. He could feel anxiety tightening inside his chest. *Count backward from ten...nine...eight...seven...* The object pressed harder against his throat... *Six...five...four...* A few more seconds and he'd be fine... *Three...two... one.* There—his pulse returned to normal. The military had taught Dylan to adjust his body's response to stress. He took in a deep breath. The pressure around his neck eased. Whatever they'd used was too soft and too thick to be a cord. He was most likely dealing with a rope of some sort. And that was about the best news he'd gotten so far. He continued working his hands against the tape, trying to break free.

Still no luck there.

The next thing he knew, he was being pushed off the

table and onto his feet. His knees buckled. Hands on his elbows righted him and kept him upright. With a bag over his head and his arms bound behind his back, he immediately thought that he was being prepared for execution. Nothing Dylan hadn't been exposed to before. Dylan walked through the scenario in his mind to prep himself for it. They'd most likely take him out to the field and then force him onto his knees. There'd be bright lights in his face once the bag came off again, loud cursing and threats.

His adrenaline spiked thinking about it. Good. He'd rather have that happen now while he was being forced to walk than once the bag was off. They'd probably get in a few more jabs, especially if Bearded had anything to say about it.

He pictured himself being calm, watching for an opportunity to fight back. If any one of them got too close with a gun, Dylan could disarm the guy in two seconds flat. If there were still only three of them, the odds were decent that he'd be able to take them down.

Without the free use of his arms and hands, that would be tricky but not impossible. He tried to move his hands again. Nothing. His wrists were wrapped up too tightly.

Most likely, this was all a big bluff. Dylan had to consider every possibility. He had to prepare for the scenario that they were actually going to execute him, as well. He thought about why they'd shoot, and his muscles coiled as anger burned through him. They would have to have Samantha. That would be the only reason they no longer needed him. Plus, since he'd seen their faces, they'd have no choice but to do away with him. He'd committed all three to memory. Bearded was the tallest and scruffiest. The other two looked as though they could be brothers. There was only an inch of height difference between them. Both had bright red hair and blue eyes. Bright Guy One had tattoo arm sleeves and his theme seemed musical. There were staffs filled with notes running up his right forearm. On his left were instruments linked together. The other Bright Guy had a snake eating a bird while wrapped around a tree.

Dylan could identify all three men and testify against each one. If a smart prosecutor did enough digging, it couldn't be that difficult to tie them to their boss.

So, basically, whatever was about to happen wasn't looking good for Dylan. He needed to think his way out of this situation. Based on the grip they had on his arms and the fact that no one had said anything yet, he didn't figure these guys would be much on conversation.

With one on either side of him, flanking him, he guessed the third was walking behind and had his gun pointed at Dylan's head. If that man happened to be Bearded, then he wouldn't need much encouragement to pull the trigger.

But they'd said they had orders. *Great.*

He'd given up on the chance that he'd be taken to the guy in charge.

A door opened and then shut behind them.

The ground underneath his shoes was forgiving, which told him that he was no longer walking on concrete. So they'd taken him outside and not into another room. Okay, this was bad, but Dylan had been in precarious situations before and managed to get out alive.

"On your knees," one of the guys shouted. "Where is she?"

Yeah, this was about to be a picnic for four.

Dylan shrugged.

"Boss just wants to have a conversation with her."

"He ever hear of a cell phone?" Dylan shot back.

Any second now they'd be jerking off his head covering and then he'd be blinking his eyes to adjust to the bright light. Guns would be pointed at him, so he needed to ready himself for that.

Since they hadn't shot him already, he held on to the hope that Samantha was still at the barn and didn't answer.

He didn't want to think about how much he missed her. Or the fact that he couldn't get her out of his thoughts. Maribel was already his kryptonite, so he didn't want to have to worry about another human being. Bel was enough to think about.

Dylan tensed and relaxed, trying to get his muscles to stop from knotting up on him. His arms were already cramping. Even if he could get the bindings off, he doubted it would do any good. Then again, adrenaline did funny things to the body. And just thinking about Samantha's and Maribel's safety had his pumping.

"You think you're funny?" The toe of a boot nailed Dylan in the ribs.

"I'm a freakin' comedian."

"I bet she's gone. He doesn't know anything," one of the men said.

Ready for the bag to be pulled off, he tensed when hands gripped his biceps and he was hauled up and then tossed onto hard metal. A latch clicked, like a gate.

The sound of doors opening and then closing came next. Car? Truck?

He couldn't be sure until the engine roared to life. Then he was certain that he was in the back of a Bright Guy's truck.

Excitement trilled through Dylan's body. There were

two scenarios possible here. Either he was being taken out of town for a body drop or he was going to meet the guy in charge. He kept working the bindings against his wrists, trying to get a little wiggle room.

Nothing was happening there.

Dang. Whatever material they'd used was unyielding. It was wide, covering at least three inches of his wrists. It was sticky, so his earlier assumption that it was duct tape was probably spot-on.

So far, the roads were bumpy. The truck had kicked up dust, so the warehouse he'd been taken to had to be on the outskirts of town.

Dylan made mental notes about everything he remembered. Didn't help that his head was still splitting from one helluva headache. Everything might be riding on what he thought, heard or felt.

So he shoved his pain to the back burner and listened. They were traveling fast down the rutty road. Air cooled his skin. Even though it was the hot part of summer—eighty degrees when he went to bed, eighty degrees when he woke the next morning—the draft was nice.

He counted in order to track how long they'd been driving.

By the time they stopped, they'd been on the road at least thirty-five minutes. The roads had smoothed and then gotten bumpy again.

They could've been anywhere. He hadn't heard anything to distinguish the area they were taking him to. No noises typical of a city at night either, so they must've stuck with the country.

His shoulder hurt from being bounced around. It battled with his head for the body-part-in-the-most-pain award.

The gate opened and he was suddenly being dragged out by his ankles. *Damn.*

A set of hands gripped his body, pulling him by his shirt, but he bounced on the hard dirt anyway.

Someone stepped over him.

"Boss says you have twenty-four hours to find and bring the lady to the drop spot and then he'll give your daughter back. Time's ticking."

"He hurts my child and it'll be the last thing he does," Dylan ground out.

"There are other ways to take care of your daughter without putting a hand on her."

The noose loosened around Dylan's neck and the canvas bag was jerked off. Dylan blinked, trying to gain his bearings as he lay on his side in the dirt. Not exactly the best vantage point. The pickup truck was behind him. It'd be all too easy for one of the guys to put the gearshift in Reverse and back right over him.

A cell phone was shoved in his face.

There was a picture of Maribel standing in the corner, arms folded, with a copy of the day's newspaper. Her stubborn streak could get her in trouble with these bastards. Rage boiled through Dylan. He reminded himself to stay calm. She was healthy, alive and it didn't look as if anyone had laid a hand on her. As long as they kept it that way, they were cool. None of those men wanted to see the hell Dylan would bring forth if anything happened to Maribel.

"You want her back in one piece. Do as the boss says," Bearded said.

Dylan surveyed the guys. Two were to his right. Bearded was to the left. He was the only one looking away. The big man didn't seem to like the idea of a little girl getting hurt. Did he have kids of his own?

"Let me tell you something and, please, do me a favor and take this back to whoever's in charge. If anything happens to my daughter, if she so much as snags a fingernail while in your boss's care, then every last one of you had better sleep with your eyes open for the rest of your lives, because there is no length to which I will not go to personally destroy you and everything you love. And if anything happens to me, I have half a dozen friends who will see the job through on my behalf. That you can count on," Dylan ground out.

Something flashed behind Bearded's eyes. Since it didn't faze him to beat the heck out of Dylan, the man had to have a family.

The other two didn't flinch.

"Forgive me if I'm not scared," one said, making his body tremble in order to mock Dylan. "You're not exactly in a position to dish out threats."

"My name is Dylan Jacobs. Remember it. Because if this goes down wrong, I'm the man who will put you in your grave."

One of the men reared his foot, ready to kick, but Bearded stepped in between the guy and Dylan, putting his hand against the guy's chest. "Let's go. Like you said before, this dude is all talk. He's not worth it. We did what we were supposed to. Now let's grab some food."

"Whatever." The guy blew out a sharp breath, turned and moved to the passenger side of the truck. The other one took the driver's side.

"Where are you keeping the old man?" Dylan shouted toward them. He couldn't go back without news about Samantha's father.

Bearded turned his back to Dylan and started toward the truck. The big guy paused, and then a small shiny metal object landed near Dylan's head.

Out of the side of his mouth, Bearded said, "The old guy is with your daughter."

Dylan was already scooting toward the ditch. He managed to palm the object as he rolled out of the way. Giving those guys an easy target wasn't in the plan today. Besides, the driver would've been all too happy to put some tire treads on Dylan's chest.

Feeling the oblong object with grooves down the side, Dylan realized he'd been given a pocketknife.

He had no idea why Bearded was being so generous. The other two seemed intent on making things as difficult as possible. As it was, Dylan was stranded on the side of the road with no idea where he was or how to get back to Samantha. He had no phone and no way to get word to Samantha that he was safe. She had to be worried sick by now, and his biggest fear was that she'd go out looking for him. Based on the position of the moon and the time of the year, he figured it was before midnight. He opened the knife and cut his hands free. Then he sat up, rubbing his sore wrists to get the blood going again.

If it was close to midnight, he'd been knocked out in that warehouse for a couple of hours.

There were two things saving his sanity right now. Maribel's picture, for one. She might not be happy, but she was fine. They seemed to be taking good care of her. *They'd better be.*

And he knew Samantha was safe as long as she stayed put. They still wanted her and they were willing to do pretty much anything to get her, including set him free.

Dylan hoped like the dickens that she'd stayed inside the barn, where she was safe. It would be just like Samantha to take off looking for him, and he'd been gone too long already.

Samantha woke to the sound of the door opening. She bolted upright. "Dylan?"

It was late and she'd almost gone looking for him. A foreboding feeling had returned her to the office. No way did she want to jeopardize the innocent lives tangled in this web.

"I'm here." His voice was gruff.

All she could see was his silhouette with the light streaming in from behind him. He was limping.

She pushed off the sofa and was at his side in a second. "You're hurt. What happened to you?"

"Get me to the couch." He put a little of his weight on her for the rest of the walk. There was so much blood on his shirt.

In the soft light, she could see bruises on his face. There was a cut over his right eye.

"What did they do to you?" She pushed back the tears threatening, grabbed the first-aid kit and bent down in front of him. She immediately went to work on his injuries.

First she cleaned the cut with fresh water and a wipe. He flinched at her touch.

"I ran into a few of his guys." He sat with his elbows on his knees, looking down.

"What did they put you through?" She blotted antibiotic ointment on the cut, fighting the panic that he was truly hurt.

He pulled back and caught her wrist in his hand. It was then that she saw how red his were.

"I let them take me, thinking I'd end up wherever Maribel was." He loosened his grip on her wrist and pulled it to his lips, placing a kiss on the soft skin. "Sorry. Keep going."

Then he released her hand altogether.

She ignored the sensations pinging through her body and instead focused on the degree of his injuries. He was back, safe. She could only imagine what had happened to him.

"Does this hurt?" She gently blotted his cut again.

He sucked in a burst of air but shook his head.

"You're a terrible liar," she said, placing gauze over the wound, then taping it to hold it in place. She wiped his face with a clean cloth, being extracareful on the spots where bruises were beginning to form.

His hands closed on the sides of her waist, and he bent forward until his head rested on her stomach.

"They're going to hurt her if I don't figure out a way to find them in the next twenty-four hours."

"What did they say, exactly?" She ran her hands through his dark hair.

He lifted his gaze to hers. "First of all, she's with your dad."

Relief washed through her. "They're both safe?"

"As far as I know." He caught her eye and she knew he was being completely honest. Besides, it wasn't like Dylan to sugarcoat things. She could trust what he said. "They want a trade."

"That could work. Same meet-up location?"

"No way. I'm not having it. They kill you and she's dead. So is your father."

"And what will they do if I don't show?"

"You don't come and they'll kill one of them, or both, which might just be a threat. We can't be sure they'll follow through."

"You really want to take that chance?"

"No. Of course not. But we're not exactly dealing in ideal circumstances right now." He bowed his head for a second. "The other choice is that we get evidence against

Charles Alcorn and force his hand. We have to bring the fight to his doorstep."

"It sounds too risky. What if it's not Alcorn? Then we have nothing."

He slanted a look at her.

"Did they give you any way to contact them?" she asked.

He shook his head.

"Would you tell me if they had?" she asked, guessing she already knew the answer to that question.

He just stared at her, didn't speak, didn't make a move to speak.

"I thought as much."

"They didn't, though. I'm being honest about that, which reminds me—I have to call Jorge."

She watched as Dylan moved to the desk and called his friend, explaining that they'd gotten his cell phone and he'd had to pick up a pay-as-you-go phone from the convenience store. She couldn't hear what was being said on the other end of the line, but Dylan nodded his head and thanked his contact before returning to his spot on the couch.

"Dylan, listen to me. I would do anything to get your little girl back. If they want me, let them take me. I'll go alone. I'll tell them that I told you everything and that you're going to the police if I don't walk out of there with your daughter."

He didn't immediately respond. Instead, he seemed to carefully consider it. "No."

"Not so fast. This could work."

"I won't trade one life for another." There was so much torment in his gaze that it momentarily robbed her breath. "Besides, we don't know if it will work. I've thought through every scenario, and every single one carries too much risk. I won't allow anything to happen to you."

He might not be able to choose between her and his daughter, but she certainly could. Nothing was worth that little girl's life. Samantha would figure out a way to make the trade on her own if she had to.

"I know where they'll be in twenty-four hours. That's more than we've managed to figure out so far."

"How do you know Maribel is okay?" She didn't want to ask but she had to be sure.

"They gave proof of life."

When she responded by lifting her eyebrow, he added, "Her picture with today's paper."

"Why would someone know to do that?"

"This isn't their first rodeo. They also had access to an out-of-town warehouse and I'm guessing they move 'product' through there." The way he emphasized the word made her think he couldn't say what they really moved—children.

More children.

"Did they say anything about my father's health?"

"No."

"What about a picture of him?"

Dylan took in a sharp breath. "We're going to get them both home safely. We'll figure this out. You have my word."

She wanted more from him than that and he seemed to sense it. He pulled her closer until her body was pressed against his and she could feel warmth radiating from him. She leaned into it, into him, and let him guide her mouth to his.

There were about a thousand reasons why she shouldn't allow this to happen, not the least of which was that her feelings seemed to run deeper than his. It had been all too easy for him to push her away every time they got close. Even though logic said the pull between them was strong enough for him to keep coming back, it also said that past behavior was the best predictor of the future. Or, as she liked to think of it, when someone showed her who they truly were underneath it all, she believed them.

Was there a strong attraction between her and Dylan? Sure. They both had to feel that same electric jolt every time they were near each other or their skin touched. Did she want him to kiss her? Yes.

She parted her lips to give him better access, because all she wanted in this moment was to feel the comfort of his arms around her, as they were, and the safety she felt with him this close. No one had ever had her back like Dylan. It was a feeling she could get used to, *wanted* to learn to depend on.

And even though everything inside her said he wanted more than friendship, she'd be stupid to let this attraction get out of hand. Precisely what was happening.

She pulled back and then stood.

"I think we should figure out our next move."

"Right." A hurt look crossed his intense green eyes, and she couldn't say that she blamed him for feeling that way.

But she'd already touched that stove how many times? And it was always the same result. They got close and he pulled back. At least Dylan was more honest than Jude from college. He'd betrayed her in the worst way, taking what he wanted from her and then making sure he was getting it everywhere else he wanted, too. All the while, she'd happily played into his sob story about how hard it was to be a student and a single father.

Dylan never complained about parenthood, or anything else, for that matter, but that still didn't change the fact that he would never seriously entertain his feelings for her. He was one of the good guys—she knew that.

And that would make walking away from him hurt like hell.

Chapter Thirteen

"Rebecca brought food earlier," Samantha said as she sauntered across the room toward the minifridge. Nervous energy had her needing to move around.

Dylan sat there for a long moment, thinking about what had just happened. The pull he felt toward Samantha was incredibly strong. He chalked it up to their history, their friendship and the craziness going on around them that only the two of them could understand. But was it something else? Something deeper than circumstances?

And maybe a better question was…could it be more?

Another time, another place, and they might have had a shot. His existence was a wonderful chaos by the name of Maribel. With that little girl in his life, he didn't have time for anyone else. Period.

As long as he was playing "what if"—*if* the circumstances had been different, then Samantha would be exactly the kind of woman he'd be interested in pursuing a relationship with.

This back-and-forth without going anywhere needed to go, and she was clearly just as tired of it. Good thing one of them had the presence of mind to keep them honest.

Samantha stood in front of him not two feet away, staring with a bowl in her hand. "Hungry?"

"Nah. I'll grab a power bar. You go ahead and eat."

"What were you thinking about just now?" She eased onto the couch next to him.

"How crazy life can be."

"One minute you think you know where you're going, what you're doing, and then wham! A curveball," she agreed. She took a bite and chewed.

"I'm proud of you, Samantha. You've been through hell and back but you're still standing. That takes guts," he said. "No matter what happens, I hope you know you can always count me as a friend."

"And what about you? It couldn't have been easy to wake up a father one day. I've seen you with your daughter. You're a great dad."

"Thank you," he said and meant it. "I had no idea that parenting was mostly about second-guessing yourself all the time."

"I can only imagine," she said. "Think about all the stuff we used to do to our parents and your grandmother when we were kids."

"Yeah, she might've been too strict, and that presented a whole different set of problems, but I'm pretty much thinking she was a saint for taking me in when she did. She was still working her way toward retirement when I showed up. I'm sure she hadn't planned on that financially." Had the strain been too much for her? Was that why she'd pulled back on the leash harder? The two of them had clashed like soap and vinegar.

"I had four fathers after my mother died."

"Must not have been easy being the baby."

"You remember that I had to sneak out to do anything. I was way too overprotected, and that wasn't good, either.

I didn't get a chance to make my own mistakes, because there was always somebody there to guide me in a different direction before things went haywire." She paused. "Either extreme isn't good for a kid."

"I try to walk the middle ground with Maribel."

She shot him a look.

"What?"

"I've seen you. You're not middle ground, Dylan."

"Okay, fine. You got me there." He held up his hands in surrender. "More than anything, I just want her to know how much I love her and want her. Everything else seems so much less important." Dylan paused, his emotions getting the best of him. Truth be known, all he really wanted was her to be there with him.

"We're going to get her back. They won't hurt her as long as I'm out here, just like you said. I won't let them get to me." She leaned into him, shoulder to shoulder, and those thousand little fires lit inside him again.

"That's why I've been thinking we have to find them first."

"Okay, what do we have to go on? Anything that we haven't already thought of?" She set the bowl on the side table next to her.

"I've been racking my brain. All I keep thinking about is Maribel's face in that picture. She looked confused but brave. I can't let her sleep another night away from home, Samantha."

"What else was there in the background? Where was it taken?"

"Good questions. She was standing in the corner of a room. I have no idea where but it didn't look like a house. It wasn't a warehouse, either. The lights were bright and there was a wooden rocking horse to her left."

Samantha's jaw went slack. "What did the horse look like?"

"It was black with white spots and a white saddle. Looked as though they'd pushed it over toward her to get her to—"

"Hold on a second. That's my horse. We have to go to the store."

Dylan was already on his feet. "Maybe I should go alone."

"Not a chance. You need me with you, and I have a key. Just get me to my dad's house so I can get it."

"I doubt this is a trap. However, we need to be careful." Taking Samantha anywhere out in the open was a huge risk. All anyone needed was a clear shot and it would be over. They already had two of the three puzzle pieces in check. They didn't see Dylan as a threat, which was why they'd let him go. Then again, they didn't know him.

Dylan called Brody to get permission to borrow his truck.

"Brody said there's an extra set of keys in the top desk drawer," Dylan said to Samantha.

She retrieved them and followed Dylan to the door.

They listened as they leaned against the door, quietly, so that the only sound that could be heard was their breathing and the occasional neigh, snort or whinny of a horse or shuffle of hooves.

After turning off the tiny light in the office, Dylan took Samantha's hand and led her outside. Keeping their backs against the barn, they moved in perfect unison to the truck.

Once they got on the road, with any luck, people would confuse them for Brody and Rebecca.

Dylan moved into the driver's seat, put the key in the

ignition and started the truck. A few minutes later, they were on the road headed toward town.

The Turner house was a few blocks from the hardware store. Dylan had never been inside Samantha's childhood home. Her brothers never would have allowed it.

"What was it like growing up with all those men in your life?"

"I couldn't get away with much."

"Is that a good or bad thing?" Sounded pretty darn good to him about now.

"Both. I rebelled from being smothered, so you don't want to go that route. That's why I sneaked out, and looking back, I realize that was such a stupid thing for any of us to do."

"Getting out, being with you guys, kept me sane. Or at least somewhat," Dylan said, half smiling.

"Don't get me wrong—I loved it. Spending time with you guys made me happier than I'd ever been. If everything hadn't backfired, it would've been a great thing. But we left ourselves vulnerable because no one knew what we were doing."

"Except people playing the game," he said.

"Why does everything have to circle back to that horrible summer?" she asked, her tone heavy.

"I wish it didn't."

She just sat there and stared out the window for a long time. "To answer your question, I think you're a terrific dad. You don't have to worry. Maribel will be loved, and that's the best you can really do for a kid."

"I failed her mother and I'm scared I'll do the same with her."

"You BELIEVE THAT, don't you?" Samantha looked at Dylan, at the anguish on his features, and her heart did a free fall. From what she'd been told, none of this had been his fault. Did he always carry the weight of the world on his shoulders? Was that why he'd been so tough all those years ago? He'd had to be? She'd been the complete opposite. Everything had been done for her, handled for her. Trevor had walked her to school and Brent had picked her up.

Looking at Dylan now, she could see how absolutely alone he must feel in bringing up his daughter by himself.

"I should've known that Lyndsey needed me. I was a selfish bastard. All I could think about was how great it was to see her when I was on leave. I had no idea what she was going through on the inside. She must've felt rejected and abandoned by me to do what she did. Then to suffer her sickness alone with a toddler..." His voice trailed off. "The news about her leaving town was like lightning striking on a clear blue day. I had no warning, and it feels as though if we were really that close, shouldn't I have realized something was up?"

"No one can know how someone else is feeling unless that person is willing to share. You're not a mind reader, Dylan." A little piece of her heart opened up at the thought that he was confiding in her. Dylan didn't talk to anyone about what he was feeling.

"You're mad at me. I keep frustrating you. I know that because I can read you, Samantha. With her, I had nothing to work with."

"We've known each other forever, Dylan. I'm not someone you met six months ago. We have a long history together. But let me ask you this. How did you really know I was angry?"

"Your lips thin just a little when you're mad. Not much. And you frown when no one's talking. You get quiet and go inside your head. You're a thinker and you've always been that way," he said.

Samantha wasn't sure if she liked how well he seemed able to read her.

"Okay. My turn. You're confused. You have feelings for me but you'd never let them surface. You put everything else above those feelings because they scare the hell out of you."

Dylan grunted. "I don't do afraid."

"If that's true, then you're just a jerk, and I know better than that."

He sat silent for what felt like an eternity as they slipped into town, heading toward Main Street.

"You asked about my nickname before. I'm not proud of it. That's why I didn't want to tell you."

"Aren't nicknames supposed to be embarrassing?"

"Yeah, well, this one has to do with some of the more immature activities we participated in while on leave."

"And?"

"Mine has to do with how fast a woman's bra tended to unsnap when she was alone with me."

"Oh." Snap-trap. It made sense now.

He seemed to be waiting for more of a response from her but it took her a minute to process. He added, "I was young and stupid."

"And good-looking," she said. It was no surprise women would throw themselves at Dylan. He was the very definition of *strong, hot male*. Although she didn't like hearing how many— Jealousy coursed through her. But he was opening up a little more to her. He was trusting her with information that obviously embarrassed him. She couldn't fault him too much for his past mistakes.

Maybe that explained why he was so cautious with her now.

"Your dad's place is a few blocks away. To be safe, I'll park behind the restaurant. We can walk from there. Take alleys."

"It'll be better to take Oak instead of Maple. No dogs," she said.

They got out and he fell in step beside her.

At the end of Oak, he stopped. "I just want you to know that I heard what you said in the truck and I apologize. I have some serious thinking to do."

With that, he urged her to keep moving.

What was she supposed to do with that information?

Chapter Fourteen

Tension corded Dylan's muscles with each step closer to the hardware store. They'd retrieved her store key in silence. Samantha deserved an explanation. She was right. He'd been hot and cold with her and it had nothing to do with his feelings. They were always hot. Too much like an out-of-control forest fire for him to be comfortable.

There was a connection between the two of them that he hadn't experienced with anyone else, not even Lyndsey.

Was it because of shared history? Possibly. And something else, too. Something more primal. Something that he didn't have to work at. He just understood Samantha, and it seemed to go both ways.

But he couldn't think about that right now. All he could focus on was getting Maribel back home safe and sound.

His fists curled and adrenaline pumped through him as he thought about the possibility of facing down the jerks who'd taken his daughter. She'd been photographed in the back room of the hardware store, so they needed to enter through the front.

"What about an alarm?" he asked.

"I know the code."

"The noise will give us away if someone's inside, and we don't want that."

"Good point." She stopped and he took her hand in his. Her fingers went still, then wound through his.

Dylan led her around toward the back of the building. A single light fixture stood sentinel over the metal door. The back parking lot was completely empty.

Gravel crunched underneath their shoes as they moved to the side of the building. Downtown, stores were linked together by a common wall. The hardware store sat at the mouth of the alley and anchored the strip.

He leaned his head at the crack of the door, listening for any sounds coming from inside the stockroom.

All was eerily quiet—the kind of quiet where even the air felt stale.

After ten minutes, Dylan was certain that if anyone was in the building, they weren't awake.

He took Samantha's hand again and moved down the side of the building toward Main Street and then turned right. The windows were dark. There was no sign of movement inside.

Samantha squeezed his fingers and then angled her head toward a blinking red dot on the wall.

"The alarm isn't armed," she said.

There were no signs of forced entry, either, in back or in front.

"I want to go in first." He didn't admit his worst fear that her father and his Maribel might be inside, dead. Anger burned in his gut. Dylan blocked out the possibility. *They're safe. They'll be home tonight.* Those were the only two thoughts he could allow in his head. He couldn't afford to think any other way.

Samantha unlocked the wooden door that was half-glass. The hours of business were posted on the top half.

Other than that, the hardware store had two bay windows with *Turner Hardware* etched in white letters on one side.

A bell tinkled as Samantha opened the door. She winced. "Shoot. I forgot about that."

If there was someone inside, he'd know they were coming now. So much for stealth.

Samantha stepped aside so Dylan could go first.

"Wait here," he said, and then stopped. He pulled out his Glock and let the weapon lead the way. Anyone who jumped out or tried to surprise him would get a bullet between the eyes.

First he checked the aisles. Behind the counter came next. The front of the shop was clear.

He turned and waved Samantha inside.

She closed the door behind her.

The damn bell tinkled again.

There was no metallic smell in the air, and that was a relief. If anyone had been killed and brought to the stockroom, it would've had to have been recent. Bodies wasted no time starting to decay. Clean air was a good thing. In fact, it smelled like the inside of any hardware store. And it was neat. Everything seemed to have a place.

He moved toward the stockroom. Samantha was right behind him. He started to argue, to tell her to wait, but she deserved to know just as much as he did. His protective instincts had him wanting to shield her. Samantha was strong. No matter what happened, she could handle herself and then some. She'd proved it time and time again. He respected her for it.

The door to the stockroom had no lock. It was the kind that swung loosely on its hinges for an easy pass-through.

Samantha squeezed his shoulder, so he stopped.

She disappeared down an aisle and returned with a hammer in her left hand.

He smiled at her and hoped she could see him in the dim light.

As he turned, the door smacked him in the face. His body acted as a doorstop but he held his footing. The person on the other side was weaker, so Dylan braced himself and pushed back.

The battle between them held until Dylan counted to five. Then, picturing his little girl, he grunted and gave a shove so hard the other side buckled. The door swung open and Dylan used the opportunity to rush the guy.

Out of nowhere, Dylan's right knee buckled and he landed flat on his back. By the time he popped to his feet again—which took all of two seconds—the guy had pushed past Dylan and knocked Samantha down. She recovered a second behind Dylan.

Both ran after the mystery guy, who bolted through the front of the store and outside, Samantha a half step behind. Those powerful legs of hers kept her within spitting distance, even though she had to be in considerable pain, but the guy in front had a couple of seconds' advantage and could keep pace with both of them.

Dylan kept running, pushing through burning legs until his lungs felt as if they would explode. He had no doubt that if he'd been 100 percent, the guy in front of him with a medium build wearing jeans and sneakers would have been knocked out flat by now. Even a burst of adrenaline couldn't overcome the gap, because the runner had a rush of his own slamming through him.

He hopped a fence and Dylan was right there on his heels.

For a solid ten minutes, they ran.

After a good five more, Samantha dropped off.

"Keep going," she said breathlessly.

If Dylan hadn't been so close, he'd have given up.

The guy was just out of reach, and Dylan wanted more than anything to close his fingers around his neck and choke the bastard. He'd talk first, though. This guy would sing as soon as Dylan applied the right…motivation. And Dylan would have an address. Maribel would be home.

He felt torn between catching this guy, the only viable link to Maribel, and stopping to hang back in order to protect Samantha. That momentary hesitation cost him another two seconds between him and his target. *Well, hell on a roller coaster.*

The runner darted between trash cans, knocking them over. Dylan jumped in time to avoid them. It cost him another second. At this pace, no way could he make up five seconds of delay.

After the guy cut right at the next house, Dylan followed.

The first dog barked, and if Dylan was lucky, that would be the extent of it. He'd lost visual with the runner and that wasn't good. A couple more dogs sounded off, seeing which one could yap the loudest.

If he woke up the neighborhood, someone would end up calling the police. This whole situation would get even stickier.

More dogs weighed in. Was he on Maple? Wasn't that where Samantha had said the dogs were?

He kept running for at least another ten minutes, well aware that he was moving farther from Samantha and no closer to his target. She was there at the hardware store, alone.

When Dylan rounded the next house and the guy was nowhere to be seen, Dylan released a string of curse words under his breath that would've made his grandmother wash his mouth out with that deodorant soap she'd bought for him as a teenager.

Dylan stopped in the alley and listened.

He'd completely lost the runner, so he circled back and jogged toward the hardware store with a bad feeling. What if there had been another person waiting in there?

That person would have complete access to Samantha and then it would be game over. The guttural cry begging for release inside Dylan was more than just frustration that he'd never find his daughter. It was also for Samantha. And he didn't want to feel that way about anyone.

Why?

Being a parent made him feel exposed enough already. He didn't want people to have any additional ways to hurt him, and especially not in the way he'd been hurt when Lyndsey had died. It was immature to feel that she'd abandoned him because she'd died, and yet that was exactly how he'd felt. Abandoned.

Frustrated and defeated, Dylan picked up the pace. If anything had happened to Samantha—and he'd never forgive himself if it had—he needed to know, like, now.

With every forward step, his heart grew heavier in his chest and it was harder to breathe. Ignoring the pain in his calves from bursts of running, he pushed ahead, harder, faster. Getting to Samantha, knowing she was all right, was suddenly more important than air.

The hardware store was two blocks up on the right. It felt like the longest stretch of his entire run even though he ate up the ground in record time. No way could the guy have circled back and beaten Dylan to the store. And yet every possibility started roaring through Dylan's brain.

Samantha wasn't out front. Dylan wasn't sure where he'd expected her to be but maybe he'd hoped that she'd be standing on the sidewalk, waiting, so he could see her first thing.

That would be stupid, though. She'd become pretty

darn good at keeping herself alive. Only an idiot would stand out in the open, exposed. Samantha was much smarter than that. It was her intelligence that had first attracted him.

Sweat dripped down his face, his eyelids, his nose by the time his hand closed around the door handle. He turned the knob but it clicked instead. It was locked.

A few light taps on the glass and he caught sight of her silhouette moving toward him in the darkness.

Instantly, his heart filled with warmth and light. His need to hold her hit as swiftly and as piercingly as a lightning bolt straight through him.

The door swung open and she launched into his arms.

"You're back. I was so worried." She burrowed her face into the crook of his neck.

"I wouldn't go anywhere without you." He didn't want to admit just how absolutely freaked out he'd been. Not to her. Not to himself. Because needing her opened up a whole new can of worms he wasn't sure he was ready to deal with. And what he'd felt running toward the hardware store felt a whole helluva lot like need.

He walked her backward into the store and closed the door behind them.

The smell of her lilac shampoo filled his senses as her body pressed hard against him, giving him other ideas he needed to control.

For now, he'd give in to weakness and hold her.

"Did you catch him?" she finally asked, still nestled against him.

His pulse raced. His breathing was ragged. And he noticed the instant he went from heaving air to breathing in her scent. The air in the room thickened and tension coiled low in his gut. This time he needed a different kind of release. Dylan's feelings for Samantha were getting more difficult to maintain. He had to remind himself they were friends. And he didn't want to do anything to jeopardize that bond. More than anything, he wanted to be with her. And he appreciated whatever kind of connection was growing between them.

"No. He got away. I couldn't get to him in time. He was too far ahead." Dylan took a step back, frustration eating at his stomach lining.

"It's okay. We can figure out who he is anyway." Samantha held her left palm out flat, a cell phone sitting on top. "I found it here on the floor when I came back. I stepped on it, actually, and that completely freaked me out because once I realized what it was, I thought I broke it."

She pushed it toward Dylan. "It's password protected. I tried but couldn't get anything. I bet your friend can."

THE LOOK OF relief that washed over Dylan created a seismic shift on his hard features. Hard lines softened. His lips, which had been permanently formed into a frown, relaxed. His intense eyes lightened. Giving him the break he so desperately needed sent ripples of warmth and happiness through Samantha.

"We need to get this to Jorge for analysis," he said. "He'll be able to give us the name and address of the owner."

"And hopefully more than that," she agreed, starting toward the front door. She stopped when Dylan didn't follow. "I checked the back room. I didn't find anything. The computer's been tampered with, though."

Dylan nodded and they moved to the front door together. "Covering their tracks."

"I assume so."

"Where does your friend live?"

"In Garland."

"That's almost an hour away."

"I know." Dylan walked, glancing up occasionally from the phone. He pressed combinations of numbers. "It'll lock me out soon. Might have already taken our pictures."

"Cell phones can do that?" she asked, stopping at the truck.

"Some are set up to snap a shot the first time the password fails." Dylan opened the door for her.

"Maybe we'll get lucky and find pictures of who's behind all this on that phone." She climbed into the cab.

"Not with my luck, we won't," Dylan said under his breath.

Chapter Fifteen

Dylan knocked softly on the door of the small ranch-style house in the suburban Garland neighborhood. It was dark as pitch outside, but a glow came from inside and the porch light was on.

The door opened quickly.

"Thanks for remembering not to ring the bell. The kids are sleeping." Jorge wasn't at all what Samantha had expected based on his voice. He was taller and his skin was too pale for someone who lived in Texas. He had sunken dark eyes. Then she remembered what he did for a living and realized his appearance must be from staying inside so much to work on computers.

"Thanks for seeing us so late," she said, and introduced herself.

"I'd do just about anything for this guy. What happened to your face?" he asked Dylan.

"Walked into a wall."

"That was some wall," Jorge said. He turned to Samantha and stuck his hand out. "Nice to meet you. Come on in."

He stepped back and opened the door wider for them but then bear-hugged Dylan as he entered.

She followed Dylan inside.

"We need to know who owns this phone." Dylan handed the device over.

The front room had two sofas facing each other, a fireplace to the right of them. Kids' toys were scattered around, but everything else had a place. A quilt was folded over the back of one of the couches. Small frames with pictures of little kids lined the mantel.

The place had a warm feeling to it.

"Step into my office and we'll get to work." Jorge led them down a hall, practically tiptoeing past rooms with crayon drawings taped to the doors.

He didn't speak again until they'd gone into the last room on the right and he'd closed the door behind them.

"Welcome to my humble abode." He spread his arms out. The office, which was really a back bedroom converted, had a desk on which she couldn't see the top. Papers were stacked a foot high at a minimum, and where there wasn't paper, there was a manual of some type.

A cream-colored futon was positioned across from the desk.

"Take a seat," Jorge instructed. "Where'd you get this?" He hesitated, then held up a hand. "No. Don't answer that. Never mind. What I don't know, I can't testify to in court."

"I appreciate what you're doing."

"You know I'd do anything for you, bro." Jorge popped out the SIM card and stuck it into another device. He plugged that into his computer and then turned the screen around so they could see.

"He most likely had security set up on his phone if he went to the trouble of locking it," Dylan said.

"Most people do."

Not Samantha. She'd only scratched the surface of her iPhone's capabilities.

"Bingo." Jorge popped back in his chair and looked at Samantha. "That's a nice pic of you."

Samantha's face was right there, as obvious as the nose on his face, staring straight into the camera. Dylan filled the screen next. Jorge put both up side by side on a split screen.

"You two sure make a nice-looking couple." His gaze immediately bounced between them.

Neither spoke, but Samantha was pretty sure Jorge picked up on the red flush in her cheeks.

Jorge pulled up another pic, loading it onto the screen. He continued, "Does this guy look familiar?"

Dylan shook his head before turning to Samantha. "You know him?"

"Afraid not."

There were half a dozen other faces, none they recognized.

"No luck there." Samantha shrugged.

"Yeah, well, luck has never been my thing," Dylan said quietly. She tried not to notice the hurt in his voice when he spoke. She wondered if he was talking about Maribel's mother. He seemed to blame himself for everything that had gone wrong in their relationship. Samantha wondered whether, if Lyndsey had given him a chance and told him the truth—if she'd asked him point-blank what he'd intended to do—things would have worked out differently.

Knowing Dylan, he would've figured out a way to get his head around the surprise and done his level best to be there for her every step of the way. Being robbed of that chance had taken away so much from him. He'd mentally placed himself in the same boat as the parents who'd abandoned him.

When this was all over, she had every intention of telling him just that. And not because she expected anything to turn out differently between them. She realized he couldn't give her what she needed. His daughter was his focus, and that was the way it should be anyway.

"I got something here," Jorge said. "I got a number, which led me to a name. Wait a minute. Here it is. This phone belongs to…Troy Michaels." He looked up at them expectantly.

Samantha shrugged at the same time as Dylan. She figured they were repeating the same swear word in their heads, too. Neither said it, but they'd both most likely believed this guy would somehow be connected to the game. See his face and everything might finally make sense.

"Okay, we have another route. If you don't recognize the name of the guy who owns the phone, I can tell you it's a 214 number."

"That's a Dallas area code. That much I know," Samantha said.

"Okay. And he doesn't seem familiar to you at all?"

"No. But he messed with my father's computer equipment in the hardware store that he owns. This guy wanted something in the files."

"That the same system I've been running?"

"Yes," Dylan said. "You get anything?"

"Just the money connection. Deposits started being made fifteen years ago and they haven't stopped."

"They started in the summer, right?" Dylan asked.

Jorge confirmed with a nod. "I heard about that crazy stuff that happened in Mason Ridge. This is connected?"

"It would seem so," Samantha confirmed.

"Okay. Okay." Jorge rubbed the day-old scruff on his chin. He looked as though he hadn't had a good night of sleep in weeks. "Let's see who this guy's been calling, then."

He punched keys on the keyboard, then sat back.

A string of numbers showed up on-screen.

One repeated quite often recently.

"Let's just do a reverse number lookup here on Google." More keystrokes. "Private number." He laughed at the screen. "You want to play hardball, then. Okay. Let's try this."

His fingers danced across the keyboard again.

"Looks as if this guy has been calling Charles Alcorn."

Samantha looked from Jorge to Dylan. "We have proof the two are connected. People have to believe us."

Tension radiated from Dylan. "Beckett played the game with the older boys fifteen year ago, remember? Alcorn must've known his son was involved and used it to his advantage. Plus, we already know he's the only one with enough resources to pull off what he did to us in Austin."

"That's right. I didn't have much contact with Beckett, so I didn't even think about him being involved."

"Can I see that phone?" Dylan asked, his back teeth grinding.

Jorge put the SIM card back in and handed it over.

There was a missed call.

The number was Charles Alcorn's—the end to which all roads led.

"Let's see what he has to say." Dylan placed the call.

"He's probably wondering where his contact is. Maybe our guy from earlier was supposed to take the computer drive to Alcorn or check in," Samantha said.

Dylan put the phone on speaker and held it out as the line rang. "Guess he's about to get a surprise, isn't he?"

"I've been expecting your call," Charles Alcorn said.

"Or maybe not," Dylan said through clenched teeth.

"If you want your daughter back alive, you'll agree to an exchange. You know who I really want." Alcorn should sound shocked. He seemed to be expecting the call from Dylan on this line.

The runner must've let his boss know that he'd lost his phone when they'd given chase.

"Fine. Tell us where," she interrupted, knowing full well Dylan would never make that trade.

The look he gave her could've shot daggers right through her. His lips thinned.

She gave him a pleading look in return even though she knew no one would get out of this alive if Alcorn had his way.

"Tomorrow. Noon. At the fork in the road between Benton County Road and Oxford on the way into Dallas. People will be watching, and if you bring in anyone else, the girl dies," Alcorn said.

"Fine. Bring my father, too, or there's no deal."

The line went dead.

Dylan was already shaking his head. "This is a no-win situation, Samantha. I can't allow you to do this."

"How else do you plan to take him down and get your daughter back?" She sat there boldly waiting for an answer. "That girl needs to be home in her own bed. Not spending another night with those creeps."

"You can't go. They get to you and it's over." Dylan was already on his feet, gripping either side of his head with his hands. He looked at his watch. "We only have ten hours to figure this out."

"For now, we know your daughter's safe. That's all that matters." She put a hand on his arm.

"You're important, too. Can't you see that?" Standing at his full height of six foot two with muscles for days, he was a strong physical presence in the room. The man took up a lot of space and she could see how that might be intimidating to anyone who didn't know him. To her, he was Dylan. Bold and brave. Honest. Forthright. All the characteristics she respected in a man.

Jorge slipped out of the room as if aware the energy had taken on a new form, something more intimate.

"If they get to me, it's all over. I know that," she responded quietly, suddenly aware of being alone with Dylan.

"That's all you think this is about?" His face looked thunderstruck. "We've been friends a long time, and you mean more to me than just a…a…pawn to get my daughter back."

What was she supposed to do with that? Of course they were friends, but she felt so much more for Dylan than that. If that was how he classified their relationship, there wasn't much she could do about it except try not to embarrass herself again.

The way his eyes darkened when he stalked toward her and stopped not more than a foot away almost had her believing there was so much more there than friendship.

And that was just wishful thinking on her part. Dylan didn't know what to feel. He kept emotions like that under lock and key. It didn't matter how hard her heart beat with him this close or that she knew his beat hard, too. He was stubborn. He'd never allow himself to indulge in his weakness for her or anyone else. She tried not to take it personally.

"Dylan, we have to do something. You said yourself that they'll get desperate if we don't. That could lead to bad things."

"We could march over to Alcorn's front door and kick his—"

"You know he's not stupid enough to be home."

"Then, we'll get the law involved," he said.

"That won't work, either. He won't keep them where they can be connected to him. He's not that stupid. He has too many places to hide people."

"Fine. Then I'll put that bastard under surveillance." Dylan's anger was a third physical presence in the room and it obliterated all other emotions on his face.

She needed to let him talk this out before he'd be able to see reason. She could see his wheels spinning behind his eyes.

"Good idea. Call Brody. He and Dawson can do that. Or Ryan," she said. "Have people watching him that he's not expecting."

"I'll think about it." Dark circles cradled his eyes and she'd never seen him look more tired.

She walked over and stood toe to toe with him. "Even if Alcorn was keeping Maribel and my father at his house, he won't be now. He knows we're onto him and the stakes have been raised."

"Are you saying it's not worth the time to watch him?"

"No. Not exactly. I think it would be good to have someone track his movements," she clarified. "But let's not walk into a trap here."

He seemed to really consider her ideas. The pulse at the base of his throat had returned to a reasonable beat. "You're probably right."

"We should go back to your place or mine. Actually, now that I think about it, my place is better. I have security in the building. At the very least we'd be safe while we figure out our plan. We'll be twenty minutes from the meet-up spot. I have food there. All we've been eating so far to keep us going is power bars, other than the little bit of pasta I ate in the barn. We need something more substantial." She didn't feel like eating but was pulling out all the stops to coax Dylan to go to her place. Going home was something she hadn't believed possible before. Not when she'd taken off days ago with her car and a little cash. It seemed almost a lifetime ago now.

"Now that I have proof Alcorn is involved and this operation has to be bigger than just a couple of local kidnappings spaced years apart, I don't trust the sheriff, either," Dylan said, rubbing the scruff on his chin.

"I've seen them around each other quite a bit, too, when I visit Dad. It does make me suspicious of our law enforcement."

"What if they're all on Alcorn's payroll? What then?" Dylan asked.

"I don't think that's true. I could see the sheriff not wanting to rock the boat any more than he had to, maybe even looking the other way from time to time, but the FBI would've figured out if those two were in league years ago. Don't you think?" Samantha didn't want to believe that Brine could be covering for Alcorn.

"You're right. Sheriff Brine isn't smart enough to fool the FBI. So we can be relatively certain that he didn't know who was really involved fifteen years ago. Do you think he suspected his golfing buddy?" Dylan asked bitterly.

"I doubt it. If you remember, Alcorn was out there volunteering to search for Rebecca and Shane just like everyone. I think he even donated a hundred thousand dollars to the search. I know he hired private planes to watch from the skies."

"I never really thought about it before, but it would be easier to keep an eye on things if he was involved in the search party. Isn't that the reason criminals return to crime scenes? That and the high they get from reliving it and outsmarting everyone," Dylan ground out.

"True. Call me naive but I never believed it could be someone who lived in our community. How can a person look people in the eye every day knowing they did something so heinous? It gives me the creeps to think we all cried together, searched together and mourned together. And there he was, right there under our noses."

"If I had to guess, he didn't authorize Kramer to take Shane. Even dumb criminals aren't stupid enough to mess around in their own backyards," Dylan said after thinking about it for a few seconds. "And that's the reason Shane wasn't sold."

"Mind if I come back in?" Jorge peeked inside the door. His voice was low, an indication his kids were still sleeping and he'd like to keep it that way.

"Come on in," Dylan said, and then turned to Samantha. "At the very least, Alcorn's a big donor to the mayor's campaign fund. They'll protect him no matter what he's gotten himself involved in."

"True."

Dylan really looked at her. "Because you know what I'm thinking? We've known this was bigger than what we realized. It's not one kid taken here and there. Shane was the first from our town and he was the oldest until that other boy, but my guess is that they like to take younger kids. There's a huge market for them. One thing I do know is that your dad saw something he wasn't supposed to fifteen years ago and he's been paid to keep quiet ever since."

"You might be onto something there. The fact that the money keeps coming in also leads me to believe there's more going on than just what happened before." Samantha stood, hoping Dylan would take the hint that she was ready to leave.

"Kramer was part of the operation," Dylan said. "Alcorn is the brains."

"They found that kid at Kramer's house recently," she pointed out.

"True, and everyone chalked it up to him losing his own son. He was working for Alcorn all along. They were snatching kids and this guy decides he wants one for himself. Maybe he even thinks he deserves one since his son was taken from him. In the process, he brings all kinds of heat on Alcorn's operation. They're forced to stop for a while but then they get things going again."

"Eventually everything calms down until Kramer takes another little boy for himself last year, plus the fact that Rebecca refused to stop digging into the case," Samantha said.

"Right." Dylan turned to Jorge. "We're taking off."

"Okay, my friend. Just so you know, I'm heading to the meet-up location while it's still dark outside to plant a few cameras in the trees. I checked out the site and it should be easy enough to hide my equipment. I can go wireless, too. It's close enough to the city that I should be able to get a decent connection. I'll dig into Charles Alcorn's finances, too. Anything happens to you guys… I'll go straight to the feds."

"Good. Local law enforcement might be tainted," Dylan said. He paused for a beat, taking in the change in situation. "I can't thank you enough, man. You know I don't want you taking any unnecessary risks. You got a family to take care of, too, and they need you."

Everything about Dylan's demeanor—his rounded shoulders, earnest eyes—said he meant those words.

"I'm doing it for my family as much as yours. I can't let those bastards get away with taking Maribel. Besides, the two of you are my family!"

Samantha bit back the emotion building in her chest, climbing up the back of her throat, threatening to spill out of her eyes.

"You have no idea what it means to me to know you're watching my back." A look of friendship, kinship, passed between the two men.

Dylan turned to Samantha, his gaze softer now but still determined. "We can head out. I may not be able to sleep but you might."

"I'll keep working on everything you sent me. Now that I know more of what I'm looking for, I might get lucky and piece it all together. If I can link this jerk, we can turn the information over to the feds. They don't take lightly to hidden offshore bank accounts." Jorge stuck out his hand.

Dylan took it and shook, followed by Samantha.

"Thank you for everything, Jorge. It was nice meeting you," Samantha said, noticing the moisture gathering underneath Jorge's eyes. His and Dylan's relationship clearly was stronger than friendship. It was more like a brotherhood. She'd seen it all too many times with her own brothers. Mess with one and they all came running in defense. Plus, Jorge was a father. She imagined his children playing with Maribel in the past year since she'd come to live with her father. Jorge seemed almost as affected by her disappearance as Dylan. And what was happening to Dylan was unthinkable for any parent.

"Same here. When this all blows over, we should throw some steaks on the grill. We got a swimming pool in the back. Kids love it. Bring Maribel." An emotion flickered behind his eyes… Anxiety? Sadness? Pity? He seemed to quickly recover. "We'll figure this out. That jerk won't get away with this. We'll hang that SOB for what he's doing. That I promise you, bro."

"We'll get him and we'll bring her home," Dylan repeated like a mantra, a promise.

Chapter Sixteen

To say Dylan had a lot to think about was like saying bombs exploded. And that analogy wasn't too far off from what his head felt as though it might do. The drive to Samantha's place, a route he'd taken only a couple days ago, was almost too quiet. He'd switched out the truck for his SUV on the way and texted Brody to let him know where to find his pickup.

Dylan had urged Samantha to sit close to him, needing to feel her warmth, and she'd fallen asleep with her head on his shoulder.

His heart ached because he could get used to this. It felt right to have someone like Samantha in his life, on his shoulder, curled up against him. But his life was no longer about what he wanted.

Besides, it was good that Samantha was resting. She needed sleep and he needed time to come up with a plan. No way could he allow her anywhere near the meet-up site.

It wasn't until he was pulling into her parking garage that he felt her stir. "I can't believe I fell asleep for a solid hour. It felt like five minutes." She yawned and stretched. "Doesn't help much that I feel like a zombie. You know how it is when your eyes open but you don't really feel as if you woke up? It's as though you're dreaming that you're awake."

"Yeah. It's the worst. Feels like walking in quicksand."

"That's exactly how I feel right now. The only thing I know is real is how tight my shoulders are." She rolled them a couple of times as though trying to work out the kinks.

"Let's get you upstairs and into your own bed for a change." He parked in a visitor space, cut the engine and surveyed the garage. "I made sure no one followed us."

He moved quickly around the back side of the truck to open the door for her. She took his hand and he ignored the jolt of electricity running through his as soon as they made contact. This would all be over soon and he warned himself against getting used to the feeling of having Samantha next to him or the constant sexual current running between them.

Space would normally be a good thing in a situation like theirs, except the time they'd spent apart had left a cavern in his chest. He filed away his thoughts as he walked with Samantha to her condo, his hand resting on the small of her back.

Inside, after the door was secured, she turned to him. "I bought a multipack of toothbrushes two weeks ago at the grocery. They're under the bathroom sink. Feel free to use one. Shower's that way. I'll put on a pot of coffee and see if I can wake up. I'll be no good to anyone like this." She moved into the open-concept kitchen.

"I have a few calls to make first. Go ahead and shower while the coffee brews. I'll bring you a cup as soon as it's ready. Mind if I check out the balcony?"

"Not at all. Make yourself at home."

Dylan blocked out how much he liked her place and

how homey it felt, figuring he could be in a cardboard box with her and it would somehow feel just as nice. Thoughts like those were about as brilliant as waterboarding himself. There was only one thing missing in order to make his life complete at the moment and it was Maribel.

As soon as he was sure Samantha couldn't hear and no one was watching her place, he fished his burn phone out of his pocket.

Brody answered on the first ring. "What's going on?"

"How are you still awake? It's the middle of the night. I was afraid I'd wake you."

"I can't sleep, not while they have… Not until we get Maribel back," Brody said wearily. "Neither can Rebecca. We were just talking about ways we can help."

"Are you sitting down?" Dylan appreciated the support of his friends more than he could say. After basically being on his own his entire childhood, he especially respected the friends who'd become his surrogate family. And it made him even more proud that Maribel would never face the kind of loneliness he'd experienced as a young child. She would always have half a dozen surrogate aunts and uncles around. She'd be surrounded by people who loved and protected her, made her feel safe. And maybe that would provide the support she needed after losing her mother at such a young age. Maribel not having memories of him and her mother together was on him. If he hadn't been so selfish, so vocal, he and Lyndsey might've gotten married and provided a real home for Maribel.

He could beat himself up all day over that, and yet he knew the outcome wouldn't change. Lyndsey would still be dead. Dylan gripped the phone tighter.

"Yeah, why?" Brody asked.

"We caught a trail tonight and it led us straight to Charles Alcorn," Dylan said matter-of-factly.

"Seriously?" Shock was laced all throughout Brody's tone.

"I wouldn't joke about a serious accusation like this."

"No. Of course you wouldn't." When Brody repeated Alcorn's name, it sounded as if he moved the phone away from his mouth. He was most likely telling Rebecca. She would be just as stunned as the rest of them after all that Alcorn had done to find her younger brother fifteen years ago. Or, at least, all he'd pretended to do to help.

"I talked to him on the phone myself. He set a meet-up for tomorrow at noon. He wants to trade Maribel for Samantha." Dylan waited, keeping an eye out for Samantha, who'd disappeared into a back room, presumably the bathroom. The warm breeze blew on his face as he studied the blue and green etchings around buildings of the Dallas skyline.

"Rebecca just texted Ryan and Dawson. They're both up now. What can we do to help?" Brody asked. "I put you on speaker so Rebecca can hear."

"I don't want Samantha anywhere near the meet-up. It's going to take some doing to keep her away. She's convinced that she's responsible for Maribel being involved and she wants to help," Dylan said.

"I'll take her place," Rebecca offered.

"It's too dangerous. I was trying to figure out a way for one of the guys to step in," Dylan said. "Besides, you're a good six inches shorter than her."

"One of us would fit the height requirement better, but our shoulders are too broad. Alcorn's not stupid. If we have someone stand in for Samantha, they have to be believable," Brody said.

"You're right," Dylan agreed. "This will be trickier than that. I'm grasping at straws here."

"We'll put our heads together with the others and see what we can come up with," Brody said.

"Thank you. Also, I need to keep eyes on Alcorn. Can you help with that?" Dylan asked.

"Done. The guys and I will figure it out. Everyone wants to play a part in this, man," Brody said.

"You know how much it means to me to hear you say it," Dylan said, choking back the emotion clotting his throat.

"We'll get someone on Alcorn and I'll call you back with more ideas," Brody said before ending the call.

Dylan took in a deep breath and then once more called the image of him tucking Maribel into bed to his mind. *If not this night, then soon, my Bel.*

A different cavern opened in his chest, despite his best attempts to contain it. He needed a distraction. He'd been overthinking the situation and his brain was fried.

Coffee.

He'd promised Samantha a cup.

Dylan moved to the kitchen and located two mugs. He filled both with fresh brew and walked to the bathroom. The shower was running, so he knocked on the door.

"Come on in."

He did. The room was spacious. All top-of-the-line fixtures, he noted. Overall, the place was modern but warm, and he wondered if it was the color choices or if it had to do with the fact that the place was Samantha's.

The water stopped in the shower.

"I'll set the coffee on the counter." He figured he needed to get out of there, because being a half wall away from her, knowing she was completely nude, had his pulse hammering. He'd noticed right away that his body had reacted to her nearness, to the fact that she was completely naked on the other side of those block tiles.

"Okay."

He started to turn around and leave but hesitated.

She stepped around the block wall, her dark hair soaked and off her face. She looked as if she'd just risen out of a swimming pool, water beading and rolling down her face and neck.

A towel was tied loosely around her chest, and it was barely long enough to hit midthigh.

"Coffee's fresh but I'd rather you get some rest." The words came out huskier than he'd intended. He cleared his throat.

She seemed unaware of the effect she had on him, and he thought that was probably a good thing. They had a good couple of hours before they needed to kick it into gear and he hoped she'd rest while he tried to figure out his next move. His head was already pounding from hunger and exhaustion. He could live in the field for days on power bars and water. This was different. Having Maribel involved was far more emotionally draining.

"Are you sure you're okay?" Samantha slid in between him and the counter he was facing and then hopped up to sit. She took coffee from him in her right hand and used her left to trace the worry lines in his face.

He closed his eyes and took in a deep breath, keenly aware that the air in the room had become charged. Her flowery scent flooded his senses. He looked at her as he sipped his coffee. She was stunning.

"I will be."

Her finger ran along his jawline, sending awareness jolting through him. Then the tip moved over his lips, her touch lighting up all his senses. His pulse raced.

"But you do that much longer and I can't be held responsible for my actions."

She froze for a second, smiled and then traced around his ears, down his neckline. "Maybe you should let go of all that control for once."

"And ruin our friendship?"

"Let me be the judge of that, Dylan."

He shouldn't let this go any further while he still had a hint of restraint inside him. She set down her mug and then her hands came up, sliding into his hair, and she pulled him toward her until their mouths moved together. She tasted like a mix of mint toothpaste, the coffee she'd just sipped and something sweet that was uniquely Samantha.

Dylan reminded himself that it wasn't too late to stop this. He didn't do casual relationships or sex anymore. Being a gentleman, he should stop this. Now. Before there was no turning back.

He pulled away and rested his forehead against hers. They were both breathing rapidly, and he could hear her heartbeat pounding as quickly as his own.

"Dylan, I want to have sex with you."

"It's never been a matter of what I want, Samantha. We'd have been in bed by now if it was."

"I hear what you're saying and I understand the consequences."

"Good. Now you're making sense. You are so damn sexy. Believe me, you have no idea how much restraint it has taken for me to hold back."

"Then, don't." She looked him square in the eyes.

"I don't want you to regret anything you do with me."

"Is that true? Because I couldn't. I want you, Dylan. Do you want me the same way?"

Better judgment flew out the window the second she

opened her towel. He pushed in between her thighs, curled his hands around her sweet bottom and pulled her toward him until her heat pressed against his denim— denim that needed to go.

Her hands were already to his zipper before he could readjust his position and do it himself. He stood there, still, long enough for her to unzip him and free his straining length. His shirt joined his jeans on the floor.

He helped her shove his jeans down along with his boxers, and he stepped out of them and kicked them both aside.

With a groan, he pressed their bodies flush, leaving only enough space to palm her breast.

She wrapped those long legs around him and he nearly blew it right then. He wanted this to last, to be good for her, too. He had no doubt it would be amazing for him.

"It's been a long time for me. We need to slow down, take it easy."

"Or we could just do it twice." She smiled. Damn, her pink lips were sexy. Then again, everything about Samantha was smokin' hot. Her intelligence and quick wit were the foundation on which her physical beauty flourished. There wasn't much sexier than a smart and beautiful woman.

Dylan ravaged her mouth with his tongue, his need so intense he could hardly contain it.

Her hands were all over him, his face, his neck, his chest, before settling onto his shoulders, digging in with her nails.

She tasted so sweet. She pulled back long enough to bite his bottom lip, and electricity shot through him.

"You're going to destroy me."

"That's the plan," she said with a mischievous hint of a smile.

He ran his tongue across her lower lip, then down the cleft of her chin, then lower.

Her nipples were already beads in his hands and she moaned when his tongue flicked the crest of one, then the other. He took her full breast in his mouth and her entire body tensed.

Then he ran his tongue down her belly and into the warm dark curls of her mound. She leaned back against the glass and drove her fingers into his hair as his tongue slid down even farther.

Her silky thighs were still damp from her shower as he planted a hand on the inside of each and opened her legs.

As he delved his tongue inside her, she made low, sexy noises and whispered his name. Her body quivered as he worked her bud with his thumb and slid his tongue in and out of her sweet heat.

He could feel her thighs quiver as tension corded her body and her breathing quickened.

Faster, deeper, he inserted three fingers inside her again and again until she came unbanded all around him.

Satisfaction roared through him as he felt himself being tugged up. She opened the drawer next to him and pointed.

He located a condom, tore it apart with shaky fingers and slid it over his straining erection.

Her long legs wrapped around his midsection as her fingers curled around his erection, and then she brought him toward home. With one thrust, he was deep inside her. She was so wet and ready for him, stretching to take in his full length, that he had to stop and tense his body to maintain control or he'd detonate right there.

It had been a long time since he'd had sex, but no one had ever had that effect on him.

Dylan was all about control and yet he was constantly

on the edge of losing it with Samantha. She drove her tongue in his mouth and he started a slow pump, not wanting to rush, even though his body already begged for release.

Her fingers dug into his back and he thrust harder, faster.

She tightened around him and the tsunami started building. Her hips moved against his, matching his stride. Urgency roared through him.

Faster.

Harder.

Deeper.

This woman, her body, drove him to the brink. He held on for as long as he could, making sure she was satisfied first.

The second he felt her muscles clamp around him, he knew. He pumped inside her sweet heat.

He gave a guttural groan, and his release shattered inside her. And so did he.

"I love you," he whispered quietly into her neck as a thousand tiny bombs exploded inside his body all at once.

SAMANTHA LEANED AGAINST the mirror, heaving, her body still tingling. She could've sworn she'd heard Dylan tell her he loved her, but that couldn't be right and she didn't want to ruin this moment of absolute bliss a second before she had to by overanalyzing things.

In a minute, they'd need to untangle their bodies and sort out their next move.

But for now, just for this second, she needed to feel him inside her, skin to skin, his warm breath surrounding her.

They both stayed perfectly still in that flawless moment for longer than she could count.

"Are you hungry?" She moved first, and it was most likely out of self-preservation.

"I am now," he said, nuzzling into her hair, his arms tightening around her waist.

His voice did all kinds of crazy things to her insides.

"Good. I can whip up something to eat while you shower." She started to peel his arms off her.

"Do you really have to go?" He almost sounded hurt. Now she really was hearing things. Or making things up. Because not only was that the best sex of her life but she'd fallen deeper into the hole of loving him, needing him.

And that was going to hurt like hell once this ordeal was behind them and they returned to their normal lives.

It didn't help that he was already kissing her neck and her body was melting under his touch.

Way to be strong, Samantha.

And the truth was she didn't want to be resilient with Dylan. She wanted to be vulnerable with him and just feel.

"No. But stay here much longer and I can't be held responsible for my actions," she shot back playfully, echoing his earlier sentiment.

"Me, either." He leaned his head back enough to look at her, his sharp green eyes taking her in. And there was a promise in those words he didn't quite look ready to deliver on.

He pressed a kiss to her temples, her nose, her lips. "This changes things. You know that, right?"

"What does that mean, exactly?"

"I'm not sure yet." He kissed her again, tenderly this time, and her heart filled with love.

And none of that meant anything until they got her father and Dylan's daughter back alive.

"I'm going to rinse off. Want to join me?"

There was an adorable twinkle to his normally intense eyes.

She should make an excuse and retreat to the kitchen, but looking at him naked and sexy…how could she?

Samantha nodded.

He took her hand and led her into the shower.

Chapter Seventeen

Samantha hadn't been home in days. Having Dylan there made it feel complete, which was dangerous thinking. She pulled bread from the freezer and warmed a few pieces in the microwave. There wasn't much around except fixings for BLTs and tomato soup. It would have to do.

The water turned off in the bathroom.

"I put out clean boxers and jeans for you," she said from the kitchen.

Dylan walked into the room holding out the items.

"Whose are these?" He didn't look impressed.

"Trevor's. Why? You look about the same size."

"Oh. Okay." He disappeared down the hall.

What was that about? Then it dawned on her. Dylan must've thought that they belonged to a boyfriend who'd left them over.

Was that jealousy she'd seen in his eyes? More important, why did that make her feel so happy?

Dylan returned a few moments later wearing the items. The Metallica T-shirt fit snugly.

"I can't say that I agree with your brother's taste in music, but at least the shirt fits well enough." Dylan walked up behind her until his chest was flush with her back and wrapped his arms around her. He kissed her at the base of her neck, and it sent warmth running down her body, pooling between her thighs. "Mmm. You smell nice."

"So do you." She closed her eyes.

"How are you feeling? Are you tired?" His erection pressed against her, sending want spreading through her.

"Not too tired."

"Good. I wanted to test out your bed."

"I've never had four orgasms in an hour before."

"Well, you've never had sex with me," he said, grazing her ear with his teeth. He caught the lobe and bit ever so slightly.

Damn, this man did crazy things to her body.

"So there's even more? I really am impressed now." She set down the tomato she held before turning around to face him. She looped her arms around his neck.

He picked her up and took her to bed, where they made love slowly, sweetly.

"WE SHOULD EAT and check in with the others," Dylan said.

"I'll get dressed." She made a move to get up.

"Not so fast." He caught her and tugged her back into his arms, where he was all warmth and strength.

She kissed him and she honestly couldn't remember the last time she'd felt so happy. Nothing about their current situation should have made her feel safe, and yet she felt just that. Her warning bells sounded and she needed to put a little space between them. "We probably shouldn't get too comfortable."

He looked a little hurt by the barb but he didn't immediately say anything. He just loosened his grip so she could get up.

When he strolled into the kitchen five minutes later,

she had everything heated and ready to go. Thank heaven for microwaves.

They ate in silence but Dylan had returned to his heavier thoughts. She could see it in the worry lines in his face, in the heaviness in his eyes.

After finishing up the snack and doing dishes, Dylan motioned for her to sit by him on the couch. She snuggled up against him and closed her eyes. She had never felt so close to another person, so comforted as when Dylan's arms were wrapped around her.

That was the thing she remembered thinking before waking with a jolt.

The sun was already up, peeking through the crack in the closed curtains.

"Dylan?" She glanced around. No sign of him. She listened, hoping to hear water running in the bathroom.

The place was quiet.

She scrambled to her feet and checked every room.

Had he just left without her?

Her heart pounded in her chest at the thought of not knowing what was happening. It was eight o'clock in the morning, so the meet-up wasn't for another four hours.

The door handle jiggled and Samantha's back tensed, fear coursing through her. She dropped down behind the couch and grabbed the metal candlestick on the side table. If she needed to defend herself, she would fight to the end.

It was as if the air had stilled from the tension racking her body.

Footsteps fell closer and she tightened her fingers around the makeshift weapon.

"Samantha?" Dylan's voice was like a rain shower in a drought, bringing nourishment to parched land.

"Right here." She popped to her feet.

"I went out for breakfast and to survey the area." He was in an athletic stance, his weapon drawn. He lowered it the second his eyes made contact with hers.

"When I woke and you weren't there, I was afraid you'd gone without me." She set the candlestick down and rushed into his arms.

He tucked his gun into his waistband and set the bag of food down in time to hold her.

"I wouldn't just disappear on you. Believe me, I thought about it, but how could you ever trust me if I did that?" Dylan asked, then kissed her forehead.

Despite all the craziness going on, his reassurance brought a sense of calm over her.

"You don't want me anywhere near the meet-up and I get that. I do." She looked straight into his eyes. "Here's the thing. I have to be there. Maybe not with you, exactly, but I need to be near."

"Absolutely not." Dylan shook his head for emphasis.

"Hear me out."

He nodded but one look in those green eyes said he was reluctant to agree. She searched for the right words to convince him.

"I'd like nothing more than to be able to put this whole ordeal behind us. And believe me when I say I want to be alive to see it. I know what's at risk here and I take that very seriously. My fear is that if I'm not nearby and this whole thing goes south, the two people we love most will suffer the consequences."

"I can't allow anything to happen to you," he said, his eyes pleading. "You don't understand how deeply I mean those words."

"But I'll be safe."

"I can't guarantee that. If they get a clean shot, they'll kill you. Once you're taken care of, they'll do the same thing to your father. The entire trail leading back to Alcorn would be erased and my daughter will be killed in the process."

"There is no other choice. If I'm not there, Maribel and my father will be killed anyway." She stood her ground. "I'll take whatever risk is necessary if it means getting my father and Maribel back. I don't see any other way around it."

"What if I can't agree to this? Would you do it anyway?"

"This won't be over until the man behind these crimes is locked behind bars forever. You need me. They have to see me." She paused, waiting for a response. When none came, she added, "Do you have a better plan?"

"Send in someone for you. Make them believe it's you. Lure Alcorn to the drop and then take our families back."

"Fine. I'll stay with Brody and Rebecca. But you have to let me be there. I'm just as vulnerable here alone as I would be with you guys."

He didn't voice an argument but she could see the battle going on inside his head. She could also tell that she was getting to him.

She pressed up on tiptoe and kissed him. "We can finish this, figure out what *this* is when my father and Maribel are safe again."

He blew out a breath and held her tighter, his arms looped around her waist. He pressed his forehead to hers. "I meant it when I said nothing can happen to you or my daughter, Samantha. I couldn't survive losing either one of you."

DYLAN WENT OVER the mission in his head for the fiftieth time in the past half hour. There were three roads that merged at the fork, the meet-up spot, so they formed three teams aside from Dylan's. Each team would stake out a road. If they had an opportunity to intercept the "packages," they would.

If the package made it to the drop, then their friend Lisa would stand in for Samantha. Lisa would ride with Dylan. If Alcorn and his men got too close, they'd easily see that they were being tricked.

Samantha would be in another car with Brody and his team, and Rebecca would ride with Dawson. Ryan was on his own but all teams would be in constant contact.

Minutes ticked by like hours until it was time to trade Samantha for Lisa.

Dylan and his companion waited at the place where all roads merged.

The only comfort was that Dylan knew everything was being recorded on video, so even if the situation went to hell, Alcorn wouldn't get away with it. His operation would be shut down and he'd spend the rest of his life in jail.

Of course, Dylan preferred to have Maribel home, Samantha and her father safe and Alcorn in prison.

At the site, noon came and went and Dylan had a sinking feeling in his chest that Alcorn had outsmarted them. He and Lisa stayed put and waited anyway.

Twenty minutes later, word arrived from Ryan that he could confirm a car with a car seat and young child in the back had just passed him.

A few minutes and Maribel would be close enough to grab.

After what felt like an eternity had passed, Dylan's phone rang. He could see by the number that it was Brody.

"They got her," Brody said breathlessly.

"Who?" But Dylan already knew the answer to that

question. His entire world caved in all at once and his knees buckled.

"Samantha. They got her. I'm so sorry, man. We headed over to assist Ryan and they came up like a swarm around us. There had to be at least a half dozen of them."

Dylan couldn't breathe. His entire world crumbled around him. Lisa was beside him, trying to comfort him, but there were no words that could take away this pain. He'd lost the two people he loved most in the world.

"They came from every direction. I shot at least one of them but they snatched her. I couldn't shoot again without possibly hitting her. There was nothing I could do, man. I'm so sorry." Brody's voice relayed his anguish better than his words.

"Where are you?" Dylan popped to his feet.

"I'm on Benton Road."

"Which way did they go?" he asked, but he already knew, because if they went north, they'd cross paths with him. No way would Alcorn allow it.

"South. Away from town." Brody paused, heaving into the phone. "They shot out my tires so I couldn't follow."

Dylan had been so close to Maribel, so close to bringing her home. He glanced in the backseat at her stuffed animal, Rofurt. Agony bore down on him, cutting him to the core. His phone beeped. He had another call. "I gotta go. I'll pick you up."

He was already in his SUV, barreling toward Brody's drop spot.

Dylan one-handed the phone while watching the road and answered the next call with Bluetooth.

"I've got eyes on a vehicle heading toward County Road 83." Jorge's voice was rife with fresh adrenaline. "I saw Maribel in the car. She's okay."

For now. Dylan knew they'd use her to get away. As

soon as they were clear, they'd dispose of her and Samantha's father. Samantha didn't have long, either.

"That's toward Alcorn's private airstrip. We can't let him leave with them," Dylan said.

"Let me call the feds, bro. Tell them what's going on."

"Okay. I'm heading there myself, though." Dylan ended the call before Jorge tried to talk him out of it. His friend would only be wasting his breath anyway.

Dylan spotted Brody running on the side of the road. Dylan roared toward his friend and stopped quickly.

Brody hopped into the backseat. Lisa, who had been quiet up to now, filled Brody in. He pulled his weapon and replaced the clip. "Let's get those sons of bitches."

With the exchange a total disaster, Dylan prayed they'd get there in time. He had to be a good ten minutes behind Alcorn but if he made it to his plane, it would be all over. He could illegally hop over the border in hours and disappear until he bought the judge or influenced a congressman to give him pardon.

Samantha would be dead. Maribel would be…

Just as Dylan feared all hope was lost, he saw an older man running toward the road while holding a little girl. In fact…that was not just any child…it was Maribel. Dylan's heart could have exploded for how much joy he felt.

He angled the SUV toward the pair and pulled close to them. The old man held Maribel protectively as he turned toward the woods.

Dylan put the SUV in Park and hopped out.

"Mr. Turner. It's Dylan," he shouted, running toward the man holding his little angel.

Maribel turned at the sound of his voice.

"Da-da!" She smiled and cried at the same time.

Dylan held out his arms and she practically flew into

them. There were no words to describe how good it felt to hold his daughter again.

Keenly aware Samantha was still missing, Dylan turned to Mr. Turner. "We need to go. I have a tip on where they're taking Samantha."

The old man looked as though he'd aged ten years since Dylan had last seen him. Worry for a child, no matter how old, would do that to any parent.

"Thank you." Mr. Turner limped toward the SUV.

"Here. Lean on me." Dylan offered his shoulder.

At the vehicle, he climbed into the backseat with Brody's help.

"You drive," Dylan said to Brody, unable to let go of Maribel. He placed her in her safety seat and buckled her in, holding on to her the whole time. Her grip around him was viselike. He gave her Rofurt and her *Brave* doll and she immediately hugged them both to her chest.

Dylan was all too conscious of the danger of taking this group toward Alcorn. He had Mr. Turner and Maribel. It was a calculated risk he had to take in order to save Samantha.

"How did you get away from them?" Dylan asked Mr. Turner as Lisa phoned Ryan and filled him in.

"I wouldn't have without Samantha. They were trying to put us into one car when she got hold of someone's gun. She shot two of Alcorn's men before they subdued her. One had a beard and the other one was a redhead. The second one had a brother there, as well."

Bearded and the brothers. Dylan knew exactly who they were.

"She told me to grab Maribel and run." Anguish turned down the corners of Mr. Turner's lips. His eyes were burdened. "The one with the beard didn't stop me."

"We'll get her back. And when we do, I need to have

a conversation with you," Dylan said, keenly aware of the sacrifice Samantha had made to save his daughter.

Maribel was crying softly, fighting sleep.

"Hey, Bel," Dylan soothed. "Da-da is here. You're okay."

He noticed that she'd placed her *Brave* Barbie doll over her heart. He was thankful the last gift from her mother was safely in her arms.

Dylan said a silent prayer of thanks and hoped that her mother was an angel watching out for Maribel.

He thought about Samantha's unselfish act of trading herself for Maribel and her father. He was beginning to realize just how brave and devoted she was. Samantha was nothing like his own mother. All women didn't bolt when times were tough.

Damn, he also realized just how much he'd fallen for Samantha. He wouldn't rest until his family was complete—which meant Samantha being home with him, where she belonged.

"This is all my fault. I saw him that night near where the children were kidnapped. I could put him at the scene moments before it happened. Then I went to talk to him about what he might've seen and I overheard someone ask him about the kids. He told them to 'find Kramer and take care of those brats.' They discovered I was listening but not before talking about how Kramer might jeopardize their entire operation," Samantha's father said. "I should've told on him before when I had the chance. I'd been drinking too much and was scared of him."

"You aren't responsible for a criminal's actions."

"He saw me and then threatened me, my family. The only reason he didn't kill me right then and there was because of all the heat on the town. I never wanted the money but I was afraid if I didn't take it, he would hurt

Samantha. He knew how much I loved her, all of my kids. He held their safety over my head for years. Doesn't excuse what I did."

That explained why he'd been so overprotective of her, made sure one of her brothers was with her at all times.

"I wanted to make it right all those years ago and failed. When Shane showed up, I figured it was only a matter of time before the truth came out. I was ready to face the consequences of what I'd done and tell the law what I knew. But Alcorn has eyes everywhere and figured me out. You can't trust anyone. The sheriff is too friendly with Alcorn," he said. "And now that he has my baby, he'll kill her."

"Your daughter is strong. I will bring her home. You have my word." Dylan couldn't ignore the ache in his chest at the thought of losing Samantha. His heart didn't feel divided between her and Maribel. Instead, it had grown to make room for both.

He could only hope that he would get there in time.

"Do you know the shortcut through the Hatters' land that's coming up?" Dylan asked Brody.

"Yeah. I sure do." Brody cut the wheel right and the SUV bounced as he took it off road.

"If we stop before the clearing, then you guys can stay here while I hit the hangar."

"You're not going by yourself."

Dylan texted Ryan the plan as Brody parked the SUV near the tree line. The clearing was twenty-five yards ahead of them.

"I need at least one person who knows how to handle a weapon to stay back." Dylan motioned toward Maribel.

Lisa seemed to take the cue and moved to the backseat as Dylan, heartbroken at Maribel's tear-soaked face, slipped out. Luckily, his daughter felt at home with Brody and Lisa. Otherwise, no way would he have been able to leave.

They were engaging her in a game of peekaboo when he cleared the back of the SUV and moved toward the trees.

Dylan, staying low, spotted his buddy Ryan on the east side of the hangar as he came up on the west.

Dust was still kicked up from the cars that were already parked in the lot. Four men surrounded Samantha, who was fighting every step of the way. Alcorn led the pack toward the hangar.

Dylan's chest filled with pride. *Keep fighting, sweetheart. I'm almost there.*

Five against three, counting Samantha, wasn't bad odds. The men closed rank. If Dylan fired, he risked hitting Samantha.

Damn.

No way could he take that chance. *Come on, sweetheart. Give me something to work with.*

Another twenty seconds and they'd have her inside the building. If Dylan ran full force, he still wouldn't make it in time.

Samantha reared back and kicked the guy in front of her, then dropped down.

Dylan charged toward them. Ryan fired, creating a distraction.

The men's heads turned in the opposite direction of Dylan, searching the east side.

Dylan launched forward as the second group disappeared into the building. He was closer than Ryan and, therefore, had the best chance of getting there first. It went without saying that Ryan would have his back.

By the time Dylan reached the hangar, Samantha was

being forced inside an airplane. There was a pilot in place and ready to go.

Dylan couldn't allow that plane to get off the ground. He took aim and shot the wheels. The pilot ducked, and then disappeared into the back of the aircraft, closing the door to the cockpit.

"You think you got us? You think you've figured this all out?" a male voice shouted from behind the aircraft. "You don't know anything."

Alcorn.

He forced Samantha in front of him as a shield. "You're going to let us walk out of here or she dies."

Dylan held up his hands in surrender. Where was Ryan?

"Okay. I'm setting my weapon down on the floor. See." Dylan did.

"Step back!"

Dylan complied.

Alcorn stepped into view, a struggling Samantha still held in front of him, a gun pressed to her temple.

"It's okay," Dylan soothed, taking another step back to allow Alcorn passage. "I'm nowhere near my gun."

Alcorn forced Samantha to the door and then pushed her toward Dylan and ran.

Dylan dived, rolled and plowed into Alcorn's legs. Where were the other men? He already knew Bearded had been shot and at least one of his companions. Dylan couldn't worry about that now.

Alcorn tried to get up, but Dylan was sitting on his chest. Alcorn managed to point his weapon. Dylan grabbed the guy's hand and spun just as a shot fired.

Alcorn spun, fighting his way next to Dylan. A kick landed in his groin and he bit back blinding nausea in order to keep fighting. His hesitation gave Alcorn the space he needed to break free, push up to his feet and run. He kept going, unaware of the red dot flowering on his right shoulder. A few steps before reaching the vehicle, he crumpled to the ground.

Ryan entered the hangar slowly, his weapon drawn. "I got three of them outside, trying to get out the back."

"Come out of the plane. Leave your hands where I can see them," Dylan shouted to the pilot.

He complied. Dylan found rope and Ryan tied him to a chair.

Samantha was already in Dylan's arms.

"Everyone okay in here?" Ryan asked through heavy breaths as he finished his work with the pilot and called the police.

"We're good," Dylan replied, pulling Samantha into his chest, kissing her forehead. "We're more than good. Let's check on the SUV."

"I'll sit on Alcorn until the cops arrive," Ryan said.

All three moved to check on him.

"He'll live," Dylan said. "If that shot had been a little to the left, he'd be going to the morgue. I hope you enjoy prison."

Alcorn didn't respond.

The sound of sirens moved closer.

"You two get out of here so you can be with Maribel when you give your statements. I'll make sure this guy sticks around," Ryan said, digging his knee into Alcorn's back.

It took every bit of Dylan's self-control not to walk over to Alcorn and beat the man until he took his last breath.

But his daughter waited, and she'd made Dylan a better man than that.

He and Samantha made it back to the vehicle, where

everyone waited. Brody let Maribel down and she launched herself toward Dylan.

He scooped her up just in time to stop her from tripping and held on to her.

With Samantha, the missing piece of his heart, there, he felt whole for the first time in his life.

Samantha hugged them both and his heart lurched when Maribel leaned over and rewarded Samantha with a kiss.

Mr. Turner made his way toward Samantha. Maribel hugged him, too.

Dylan's cell phone vibrated, breaking into the moment.

"Hey, bro. You okay?" Jorge asked, worry in his voice.

"We're all good." Dylan paused to kiss the two most important people in his life again. "We're safe."

"I made sure the feds have the footage from today and Alcorn's account information."

"I can't thank you enough," Dylan said. "It's over."

Dylan repeated those two words.

He thanked Jorge again before hanging up.

After statements were given to the feds who showed up, Dylan loaded up the SUV and asked Brody to drive them home.

Dylan kept one arm around Maribel and the other around Samantha as he filled her in on his earlier conversation with her father. "I'd like you and your father to stay over tonight, if that's okay."

"What do you think, Dad?"

Mr. Turner nodded and smiled before leaning his head back against the headrest and closing his eyes. "It's finally over. With the other evidence and my testimony, it's done."

That night, Dylan had a lot on his mind as he placed

a sleeping Maribel under the covers. He kissed his baby, placing her *Brave* doll under the covers next to her.

Samantha was in the kitchen, cleaning up dishes.

Her father was in the guest room, resting.

And in a rare moment, the world felt right.

Dylan knocked on the door of the guest room.

"Come in," Mr. Turner said.

"I don't want to disturb you."

"I'm awake. Been in and out of sleep. It's nice to be in a bed."

"You get enough to eat?"

Mr. Turner nodded. "Best steak I've ever had."

Dylan sat next to Mr. Turner on the edge of the bed. "I'd like to have your blessing to ask your daughter to marry me if she'll have me."

Mr. Turner smiled and reached over for a hug. "You do. I'd tell you to take good care of my daughter, but based on your love for your child, I figure that's a given."

"If Samantha does me the honor of being my wife, I'll need something else from you."

Mr. Turner's eyebrow arched.

"I want you to come live with us."

"I'd like that very much," Mr. Turner said, embracing Dylan in a hug.

"Wish me luck."

"You don't need it. She's crazy about you. A father knows these things." Mr. Turner paused. "Thanks for giving me the chance earlier to explain everything I've done to protect my daughter. I made a lot of mistakes."

"Every father does." Dylan smiled as he left the room. He walked into the kitchen, unsure of himself. If he asked now, would it be too much too soon? Would she say no?

"Hey, there," he said, admiring her as she stood looking out the window. He walked over to her and took her hand, surprised at just how nervous he'd become. This time, he wasn't leaving anything to chance. He needed to put his cards on the table. "Samantha, I love you."

She smiled. "I can't imagine loving someone more."

"I know this is going to sound crazy and you might think it's too soon, but I know what I want." He bent down on one knee. "Will you do me the honor of becoming my wife?"

Samantha wrapped her arms around Dylan's neck. "I can't imagine living another day without you. Dylan Jacobs, you are my home. I belong with you. So yes. Yes. I will marry you."

"Damn. I'm the luckiest man on earth right now." He rose to his feet and kissed her. "I've always believed in family, but it was this vague ideal to me. Having Maribel show up in my life taught me what it's like to put my heart in someone else's hands. Now that you're here, I'm whole."

"I love you, Dylan Jacobs. And I want to spend the rest of my life showing you what that means."

* * * * *

*Read on for a sneak preview of FATAL AFFAIR,
the first book in the* FATAL *series by*
New York Times *bestselling author
Marie Force*

ONE

THE SMELL HIT him first.

"Ugh, what the hell is that?" Nick Cappuano dropped his keys into his coat pocket and stepped into the spacious, well-appointed Watergate apartment that his boss, Senator John O'Connor, had inherited from his father.

"Senator!" Nick tried to identify the foul metallic odor.

Making his way through the living room, he noticed parts and pieces of the suit John wore yesterday strewn over sofas and chairs, laying a path to the bedroom. He had called the night before to check in with Nick after a dinner meeting with Virginia's Democratic Party leadership, and said he was on his way home. Nick had reminded his thirty-six-year-old boss to set his alarm.

"Senator?" John hated when Nick called him that when they were alone, but Nick insisted the people in John's life afford him the respect of his title.

The odd stench permeating the apartment caused a tingle of anxiety to register on the back of Nick's neck. "John?"

He stepped into the bedroom and gasped. Drenched in blood, John sat up in bed, his eyes open but vacant. A knife spiked through his neck held him in place against the headboard. His hands rested in a pool of blood in his lap.

Gagging, the last thing Nick noticed before he bolted to the bathroom to vomit was that something was hanging out of John's mouth.

Once the violent retching finally stopped, Nick stood up on shaky legs, wiped his mouth with the back of his hand, and rested against the vanity, waiting to see if there would be more. His cell phone rang. When he didn't take the call, his pager vibrated. Nick couldn't find the wherewithal to answer, to say the words that would change everything. *The senator is dead. John's been murdered.* He wanted to go back to when he was still in his car, fuming and under the assumption that his biggest problem that day would be what to do about the man-child he worked for who had once again slept through his alarm.

Thoughts of John, dating back to their first meeting in a history class at Harvard freshman year, flashed through Nick's mind, hundreds of snippets spanning a nearly twenty-year friendship. As if to convince himself that his eyes had not deceived him, he leaned forward to glance into the bedroom, wincing at the sight of his best friend—the brother of his heart—stabbed through the neck and covered with blood.

Nick's eyes burned with tears, but he refused to give in to them. Not now. Later maybe, but not now. His phone rang again. This time he reached for it and saw it was Christina, his deputy chief of staff, but didn't take the call. Instead, he dialed 911.

Taking a deep breath to calm his racing heart and making a supreme effort to keep the hysteria out of his voice, he said, "I need to report a murder." He gave the address and stumbled into the living room to wait for the police, all the while trying to get his head around the image of his dead friend, a visual he already knew would haunt him forever.

Twenty long minutes later, two officers arrived, took a quick look in the bedroom and radioed for backup. Nick was certain neither of them recognized the victim.

He felt as if he was being sucked into a riptide, pulled further and further from the safety of shore, until drawing a breath became a laborious effort. He told the cops exactly what happened—his boss failed to show up for work, he came looking for him and found him dead.

"Your boss's name?"

"United States Senator John O'Connor." Nick watched the two young officers go pale in the instant before they made a second more urgent call for backup.

"Another scandal at the Watergate," Nick heard one of them mutter.

His cell phone rang yet again. This time he reached for it.

"Yeah," he said softly.

"Nick!" Christina cried. "Where the *hell* are you guys? Trevor's having a heart attack!" She referred to their communications director, who had back-to-back interviews scheduled for the senator that morning.

"He's dead, Chris."

"Who's dead? What're you talking about?"

"John."

Her soft cry broke his heart. *"No."* That she was desperately in love with John was no secret to Nick. That she was also a consummate professional who would never act on those feelings was one of the many reasons Nick respected her.

"I'm sorry to just blurt it out like that."

"How?" she asked in a small voice.

"Stabbed in his bed."

Her ravaged moan echoed through the phone. "But who... I mean, *why*?"

"The cops are here, but I don't know anything yet. I need you to request a postponement on the vote."

"I can't," she said, adding in a whisper, "I can't think about that right now."

"You have to, Chris. That bill is his legacy. We can't let all his hard work be for nothing. Can you do it? For him?"

"Yes...okay."

"You have to pull yourself together for the staff, but don't tell them yet. Not until his parents are notified."

"Oh, God, his poor parents. You should go, Nick. It'd be better coming from you than cops they don't know."

"I don't know if I can. How do I tell people I love that their son's been murdered?"

"He'd want it to come from you."

"I suppose you're right. I'll see if the cops will let me."

"What're we going to do without him, Nick?" She posed a question he'd been grappling with himself. "I just can't imagine this world, this *life*, without him."

"I can't either," Nick said, knowing it would be a much different life without John O'Connor at the center of it.

"He's really dead?" she asked as if to convince herself it wasn't a cruel joke. "Someone killed him?"

"Yes."

OUTSIDE THE CHIEF'S office suite, Detective Sergeant Sam Holland smoothed her hands over the toffee-colored hair she corralled into a clip for work, pinched some color into cheeks that hadn't seen the light of day in weeks, and adjusted her gray suit jacket over a red scoop-neck top.

Taking a deep breath to calm her nerves and settle her chronically upset stomach, she pushed open the door and stepped inside. Chief Farnsworth's receptionist greeted her with a smile. "Go right in, Sergeant Holland. He's waiting for you."

Great, Sam thought as she left the receptionist with a weak smile. Before she could give in to the urge to turn tail and run, she erased the grimace from her face and went in.

"Sergeant." The chief, a man she'd once called Uncle Joe, stood up and came around the big desk to greet her with a firm handshake. His gray eyes skirted over her with concern and sympathy, both of which were new since "the incident." She despised being the reason for either. "You look well."

"I feel well."

"Glad to hear it." He gestured for her to have a seat. "Coffee?"

"No, thanks."

Pouring himself a cup, he glanced over his shoulder. "I've been worried about you, Sam."

"I'm sorry for causing you worry and for disgracing the department." This was the first chance she'd had to speak directly to him since she returned from a month of administrative leave, during which she'd practiced the sentence over and over. She thought she'd delivered it with convincing sincerity.

"Sam," he sighed as he sat across from her, cradling his mug between big hands. "You've done nothing to disgrace yourself or the department. Everyone makes mistakes."

"Not everyone makes mistakes that result in a dead child, Chief."

He studied her for a long, intense moment as if he was making some sort of decision. "Senator John O'Connor was found murdered in his apartment this morning."

"Jesus," she gasped. "How?"

"I don't have all the details, but from what I've been told so far, it appears he was dismembered and stabbed through the neck. Apparently, his chief of staff found him."

"Nick," she said softly.

"Excuse me?"

"Nick Cappuano is O'Connor's chief of staff."

"You know him?"

"*Knew* him. Years ago," she added, surprised and unsettled to discover the memory of him still had power over her, that just the sound of his name rolling off her lips could make her heart race.

"I'm assigning the case to you."

Surprised at being thrust so forcefully back into the real work she had craved since her return to duty, she couldn't help but ask, "Why me?"

"Because you need this, and so do I. We both need a win."

The press had been relentless in its criticism of him, of her, of the department, but to hear him acknowledge it made her ache. Her father had come up through the ranks with Farnsworth, which was probably the number one reason why she still had a job. "Is this a test? Find out who killed the senator and my previous sins are forgiven?"

He put down his coffee cup and leaned forward, elbows resting on knees. "The only person who needs to forgive you, Sam, is you."

Infuriated by the surge of emotion brought on by his softly spoken words, Sam cleared her throat and stood up. "Where does O'Connor live?"

"The Watergate. Two uniforms are already there. Crime scene is on its way." He handed her a slip of paper with the address. "I don't have to tell you that this needs to be handled with the utmost discretion."

He also didn't have to tell her that this was the only chance she'd get at redemption.

"Won't the Feds want in on this?"

"They might, but they don't have jurisdiction, and they know it. They'll be breathing down my neck, though, so report directly to me. I want to know everything ten minutes after you do. I'll smooth it with Stahl," he added, referring to the lieutenant she usually answered to.

Heading for the door, she said, "I won't let you down."

"You never have before."

With her hand resting on the door handle, she turned back to him. "Are you saying that as the chief of police or as my Uncle Joe?"

His face lifted into a small but sincere smile. "Both."

TWO

Sitting on John's sofa under the watchful eyes of the two policemen, Nick's mind raced with the staggering number of things that needed to be done, details to be seen to, people to call. His cell phone rang relentlessly, but he ignored it after deciding he would talk to no one until he had seen John's parents. Almost twenty years ago they took an instant shine to the hard-luck scholarship student their son brought home from Harvard for a weekend visit and made him part of their family. Nick owed them so much, not the least of which was hearing the news of their son's death from him if possible.

He ran his hand through his hair. "How much longer?"

"Detectives are on their way."

Ten minutes later, Nick heard her before he saw her. A flurry of activity and a burst of energy preceded the detectives' entrance into the apartment. He suppressed a groan. *Wasn't it enough that his friend and boss had been murdered? He had to face* her, *too? Weren't there thousands of District cops? Was she really the only one available?*

Sam came into the apartment, oozing authority and competence. In light of her recent troubles, Nick couldn't believe she had any of either left. "Get some tape across that door," she ordered one of the officers. "Start a log with a timeline of who got here when. No one comes in or goes out without my okay, got it?"

"Yes, ma'am. The Patrol sergeant is on his way along with Deputy Chief Conklin and Detective Captain Malone."

"Let me know when they get here." Without so much as a glance in his direction, Nick watched her stalk through the apartment and disappear into the bedroom. Following her, a handsome young detective with bed head nodded to Nick.

He heard the murmur of voices from the bedroom and saw a camera flash. They emerged fifteen minutes later, both noticeably paler. For some reason, Nick was gratified to know the detectives working the case weren't so jaded as to be unaffected by what they'd just seen.

"Start a canvass of the building," Sam ordered her partner. "Where the hell is Crime Scene?"

"Hung up at another homicide," one of the other officers replied.

She finally turned to Nick, nothing in her pale blue eyes indicating that she recognized or remembered him. But the fact that she didn't introduce herself or ask for his name told him she knew exactly who he was. "We'll need your prints."

"They're on file," he mumbled. "Congressional background check."

She wrote something in the small notebook she tugged from the back pocket of gray, form-fitting pants. There were years on her gorgeous face that hadn't been there the last time he'd had the opportunity to look closely, and he couldn't tell if her hair was as long as it used to be since it was twisted into a clip. The curvy body and endless legs hadn't changed at all.

"No forced entry," she noted. "Who has a key?"

"Who *doesn't* have a key?"

"I'll need a list. You have a key, I assume."

Nick nodded. "That's how I got in."

"Was he seeing anyone?"

"No one serious, but he had no trouble attracting female companionship." Nick didn't add that John's casual approach to women and sex had been a source of tension between the two men, with Nick fearful that John's social life would one day lead to political trouble. He hadn't imagined it might also lead to murder.

"When was the last time you saw him?"

"When he left the office for a dinner meeting with the Virginia Democrats last night. Around six-thirty or so."

"Spoke to him?"

"Around ten when he said he was on his way home."

"Alone?"

"He didn't say, and I didn't ask."

"Take me through what happened this morning."

He told her about Christina trying to reach John, beginning at seven, and of coming to the apartment expecting to find the senator once again sleeping through his alarm.

"So this has happened before?"

"No, he's never been murdered before."

Her expression was anything but amused. "Do you think this is funny, Mr. Cappuano?"

"Hardly. My best friend is dead, Sergeant. A United States senator has been murdered. There's nothing funny about that."

"Which is why you need to answer the questions and save the droll humor for a more appropriate time."

Chastened, Nick said, "He slept through his alarm and ringing telephones at least once, if not twice, a month."

"Did he drink?"

"Socially, but I rarely saw him drunk."

"Prescription drugs? Sleeping pills?"

Nick shook his head. "He was just a very heavy sleeper."

"And it fell to his chief of staff to wake him up? There wasn't anyone else you could send?"

"The senator valued his privacy. There've been occasions when he wasn't alone, and neither of us felt his love life should be the business of his staff."

"But he didn't care if you knew who he was sleeping with?"

"He knew he could count on my discretion." He looked up, unprepared for the punch to the gut that occurred when his eyes met hers. Her unsettled expression made him wonder if she felt it, too. "His parents need to be notified. I'd like to be the one to tell them."

Sam studied him for a long moment. "I'll arrange it. Where are they?"

"At their farm in Leesburg. It needs to be soon. We're postponing a vote we worked for months to get to. It'll be all over the news that something's up."

"What's the vote for?"

He told her about the landmark immigration bill and John's role as the co-sponsor.

With a curt nod, she walked away.

AN HOUR LATER, Nick was a passenger in an unmarked Metropolitan Police SUV, headed west to Leesburg with Sam at the wheel. She'd left her partner with a staggering list of instructions and insisted on accompanying Nick to tell John's parents.

"Do you need something to eat?"

He shook his head. No way could he even think about

eating—not with the horrific task he had ahead of him. Besides, his stomach hadn't recovered from the earlier bout of vomiting.

"You know, we could still call the Loudoun County Police or the Virginia State Police to handle this," she said for the second time.

"No."

After an awkward silence, she said, "I'm sorry this happened to your friend and that you had to see him that way."

"Thank you."

"Are you going to answer that?" she asked of his relentless cell phone.

"No."

"How about you turn it off then? I can't stand listening to a ringing phone."

Reaching for his belt, he grabbed his cell phone, his emotions still raw after watching John be taken from his apartment in a body bag. Before he shut the cell phone off, he called Christina.

"Hey," she said, her voice heavy with relief and emotion. "I've been trying to reach you."

"Sorry." Pulling his tie loose and releasing his top button, he cast a sideways glance at Sam, whose warm, feminine fragrance had overtaken the small space inside the car. "I was dealing with cops."

"Where are you now?"

"On my way to Leesburg."

"God," Christina sighed. "I don't envy you that. Are you okay?"

"Never better."

"I'm sorry. Dumb question."

"It's okay. Who knows what we're supposed to say or do in this situation. Did you postpone the vote?"

"Yes, but Martin and McDougal are having an apoplexy," she said, meaning John's co-sponsor on the bill and the Democratic majority leader. "They're demanding to know what's going on."

"Hold them off. Another hour. Maybe two. Same thing with the staff. I'll give you the green light as soon as I've told his parents."

"I will. Everyone knows something's up because the Capitol Police posted an officer outside John's office and won't let anyone in there."

"It's because the cops are waiting for a search warrant," Nick told her.

"Why do they need a warrant to search the victim's office?"

"Something about chain of custody with evidence and pacifying the Capitol Police."

"Oh, I see. I was thinking we should have Trevor draft a statement so we're ready."

"That's why I called."

"We'll get on it." She sounded relieved to have something to do.

"Are you okay with telling Trevor? Want me to do it?"

"I think I can do it, but thanks for asking."

"How're you holding up?" he asked.

"I'm in total shock…all that promise and potential just gone…" She began to weep again. "It's going to hurt like hell when the shock wears off."

"Yeah," he said softly. "No doubt."

"I'm here if you need anything."

"Me, too, but I'm going to shut the phone off for a while. It's been ringing nonstop."

"I'll email the statement to you when we have it done."

"Thanks, Christina. I'll call you later." Nick ended the call and took a look at his recent email messages, hardly surprised by the outpouring of dismay and concern over the postponement of the vote. One was from Senator Martin himself—What the fuck is going on, Cappuano?

Sighing, he turned off the cell phone and dropped it into his coat pocket.

"Was that your girlfriend?" Sam asked, startling him.

"No, my deputy."

"Oh."

Wondering what she was getting at, he added, "We work closely together. We're good friends."

"Why are you being so defensive?"

"What's your *problem*?" he asked.

"I don't have a problem. You're the one with problems."

"So all that great press you've been getting lately hasn't been a problem for you?"

"Why, Nick, I didn't realize you cared."

"I don't."

"Yes, you made that very clear."

He spun halfway around in the seat to stare at her. "*Are you for real?* You're the one who didn't return any of my calls."

She glanced over at him, her face flat with surprise. "What calls?"

After staring at her in disbelief for a long moment, he settled back in his seat and fixed his eyes on the cars sharing the Interstate with them.

A few minutes passed in uneasy silence.

"What calls, Nick?"

"I called you," he said softly. "For days after that night, I tried to reach you."

"I didn't know," she stammered. "No one told me."

"It doesn't matter now. It was a long time ago." But if his reaction to seeing her again after six years of thinking about her was any indication, it *did* matter. It mattered a lot.

Continue reading Sam and Nick's story in
FATAL AFFAIR, available in
print and ebook from Carina Press.

COMING NEXT MONTH FROM

⧫ HARLEQUIN®

INTRIGUE

Available October 20, 2015

#1599 LONE WOLF LAWMAN
Appaloosa Pass Ranch • by Delores Fossen
After learning her birth father is a serial killer, rancher Addie Crockett lands in
bed with Texas Ranger Weston Cade only to learn that he wants to use her as
bait. Worse, Addie has no choice but to team up with Weston to protect their
unborn child.

#1600 SCENE OF THE CRIME: THE DEPUTY'S PROOF
by Carla Cassidy
When Savannah Sinclair is attacked in the mysterious tunnels beneath
Lost Lagoon, Deputy Josh Griffin partners with her to protect her from the
dangers of deadly secrets.

#1601 CLANDESTINE CHRISTMAS
Covert Cowboys, Inc. • by Elle James
With Covert Cowboys' Kate Rivers posing as his fiancée, billionaire rancher
Chase Marsden is determined to find the culprits trying to murder his old friend.
But will Christmas find them under the mistletoe...or escaping kidnappers and
dodging hit men?

#1602 HER UNDERCOVER DEFENDER
The Specialists: Heroes Next Door
by Debra Webb & Regan Black
Covert CIA specialist David Martin must keep a terrorist cell from using nurse
Terri Barnhart as leverage to get their hands on a biotech weapon—and falling
for her could compromise his mission.

#1603 SECRET AGENT SANTA
Brothers in Arms: Retribution • by Carol Ericson
When covert agent Mike Becker agrees to take on one last assignment—
protecting widowed mother Claire Chadwick—he never imagines that it will turn
into the opportunity to foil a terrorist attack and find redemption...

#1604 HIDDEN WITNESS
Return to Ravesville • by Beverly Long
To protect his key witness from a dangerous killer, Detective Chase Hollister
will have to pose as Raney Taylor's husband. Although their wedding may have
been a sham, Chase knows there's nothing fake about his feelings for Raney...

**YOU CAN FIND MORE INFORMATION ON UPCOMING HARLEQUIN® TITLES,
FREE EXCERPTS AND MORE AT WWW.HARLEQUIN.COM.**

HICNM1015

REQUEST YOUR FREE BOOKS!
2 FREE NOVELS PLUS 2 FREE GIFTS!

 HARLEQUIN®

INTRIGUE

BREATHTAKING ROMANTIC SUSPENSE

YES! Please send me 2 FREE Harlequin® Intrigue novels and my 2 FREE gifts (gifts are worth about $10). After receiving them, if I don't wish to receive any more books, I can return the shipping statement marked "cancel." If I don't cancel, I will receive 6 brand-new novels every month and be billed just $4.74 per book in the U.S. or $5.49 per book in Canada. That's a savings of at least 12% off the cover price! It's quite a bargain! Shipping and handling is just 50¢ per book in the U.S. and 75¢ per book in Canada.* I understand that accepting the 2 free books and gifts places me under no obligation to buy anything. I can always return a shipment and cancel at any time. Even if I never buy another book, the two free books and gifts are mine to keep forever.

182/382 HDN GH3D

Name	(PLEASE PRINT)	
Address		Apt. #
City	State/Prov.	Zip/Postal Code

Signature (if under 18, a parent or guardian must sign)

Mail to the **Reader Service:**
IN U.S.A.: P.O. Box 1867, Buffalo, NY 14240-1867
IN CANADA: P.O. Box 609, Fort Erie, Ontario L2A 5X3
**Are you a subscriber to Harlequin® Intrigue books
and want to receive the larger-print edition?
Call 1-800-873-8635 or visit www.ReaderService.com.**

* Terms and prices subject to change without notice. Prices do not include applicable taxes. Sales tax applicable in N.Y. Canadian residents will be charged applicable taxes. Offer not valid in Quebec. This offer is limited to one order per household. Not valid for current subscribers to Harlequin Intrigue books. All orders subject to credit approval. Credit or debit balances in a customer's account(s) may be offset by any other outstanding balance owed by or to the customer. Please allow 4 to 6 weeks for delivery. Offer available while quantities last.

The silence came. Addie, staring at him. Obviously
trying to make sense of this. He wanted to tell her there
was nothing about this that made sense because they
were dealing with a very dangerous, crazy man.

"Oh, God," she finally said.

Now, her fear was sky high, and Weston held his
breath. He didn't expect Addie to go blindly along with
a plan to stop her father. But she did want to stop the
Moonlight Strangler from claiming another victim.

Weston was counting heavily on that.

However, Addie shook her head. "I can't help you."

That sure wasn't the reaction Weston had expected.
He'd figured Addie was as desperate to end this as he was.

She squeezed her eyes shut a moment. "I'll get my
mother, and we can go to the sheriff's office. Two of my
brothers are there, and they can make sure this monster
stays far away from us."

"You'll be safe at the sheriff's office," Weston agreed,
"but you can't stay there forever. Neither can your family.

HIEXP1015

Eventually, you'll have to leave, and the killer will come after you."

"That can't happen!" Addie groaned and looked up at the ceiling as if she expected some kind of divine help. "I can't be in that kind of danger."

Weston tried to keep his voice as calm as possible. Hard to do, though, with the emotions swirling like a tornado inside him. "I'm sorry. If there was another way to stop him, then I wouldn't have come here. I know I don't have a right to ask, but I need your help."

"I can't."

"You can't? Convince me why," Weston snapped. "Because I'm not getting this. You must want this killer off the street. It's the only way you'll ever be truly safe."

Addie opened her mouth. Closed it. And she stared at him. "I'd planned on telling you. Not like this. But if I ever saw you again, I intended to tell you."

There was a new emotion in her voice and on her face. One that Weston couldn't quite put his finger on. "Tell me what?" he asked.

She dragged in a long breath and straightened her shoulders. "I can't be bait for the Moonlight Strangler because I can't risk being hurt." Addie took another deep breath. "I'm three months pregnant. And the baby is *yours*."

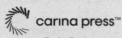